The Hostage

Samyra Alexander

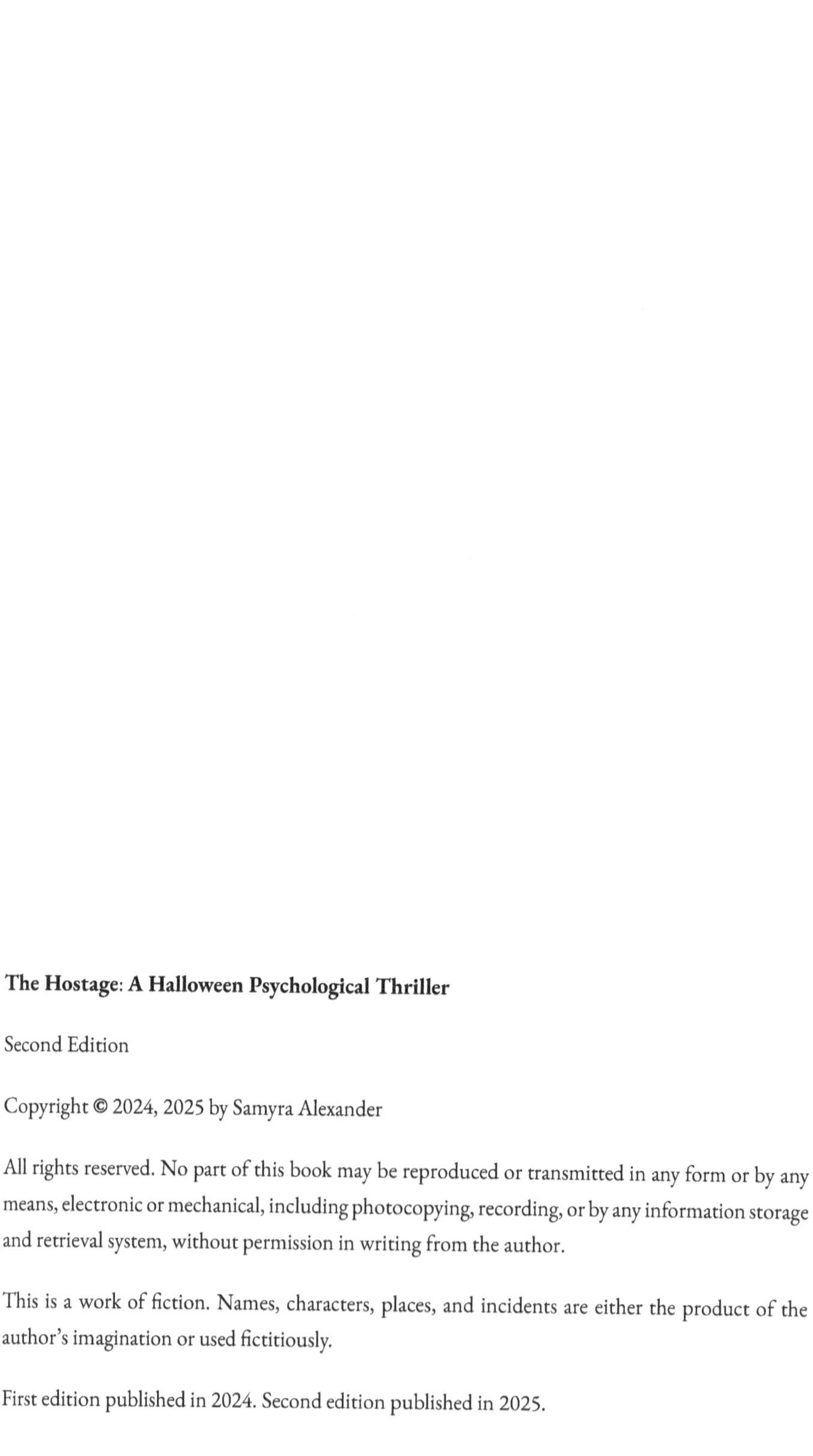

The Hostage: A Halloween Psychological Thriller

Second Edition

Second Edition Notice

This is the second edition of *The Hostage*. Revisions have been made to improve sentence structure, clarify character details, and enhance the overall reading experience. While the story remains the same, these updates were made to reflect a more polished version of the original work.

Thank you for reading.

Samyra Alexander

CONTENTS

Content Warning

This book contains depictions of murder, violence, references to sexual assault, and themes related to mental illness. These elements may trigger some readers.

ACKNOWLEDGMENTS

I AM TRULY GRATEFUL to God for the gift of storytelling. I want to express my heartfelt thanks to my beta readers, Kelly Kirkland and Amy Shakeel Randolph-Beach, as well as to my developmental editor, Author Tanisha Stewart. I also appreciate the efforts of my proofreaders, Maddy D. and Tasha Reynolds of Reanimated Editing.

I

BRANDY

BRANDY DID A DOUBLE-TAKE when she and Zane pulled up to their house at two in the morning. They had just left the club, and although many streetlights were out, Brandy saw the neighborhood's crazy man rummaging through boxes and bags scattered across their lawn. When she recognized her and Zane's belongings on the grass, she knew she was in trouble. It would only be a matter of seconds before Zane found out she was responsible. Her best friend had a temper, and she didn't know what he might do. She wasn't scared, but no one liked to argue with their best friend.

Zane turned to Brandy and said, "That's our shit he's going through. Why is all of our stuff outside?"

Brandy hunched her shoulders as if she were just as confused as he was. She needed time to think.

"I better not find out you screwed us over again, Brandy." Last month, Brandy parked in a handicapped spot, and her car got taken to impound. When she paid to get it back, Zane's expensive barber clippers were no longer in the trunk.

"I promise I didn't." She didn't like the look of disbelief he gave her, but she deserved it.

Rolling down the passenger side window, Zane cussed at the crazy guy who was missing a shoe. It was a week away from Halloween and the air was chilly. When the man picked up Zane's PlayStation, Zane brandished his gun. The man put the game system down and ran.

"I know the landlord better not have evicted your aunt, because we've been paying her fat ass good money to stay in a moldy basement." Zane put his gun away.

They had been staying in her aunt's basement for nearly a year so they could save and buy a house. Zane was obsessed with ownership because his deceased father figure, who worked at the group home where Zane grew up, always said, "Why rent when you can own?"

"I'm just as confused as you are," lied Brandy.

After Zane slammed his fist against the dashboard, Brandy wished she had obeyed her aunt's rules; if she had, they wouldn't be in this predicament. Now, Brandy's relationship with Zane would be at risk. He was the only friend she had. With Zane, she never lacked a thing. He consistently thought of ways for them to get more money, usually at the expense of others.

"Where is your aunt? She should've told you what was up so we could have gotten our stuff instead of leaving everything in the yard. I know damn well she ain't leave her things out here unattended."

"You know how Aunt Sheila is. She only thinks of herself. Who knows what happened?" Grabbing her phone, Brandy pretended to call her aunt. After a few seconds, she looked at Zane and said, "She's not answering." While he glared at her, she remained quiet, stalling to think of a solution. She knew he sensed she was at fault from how he looked at her. Turning her back to him, she texted her aunt.

I'm sorry. Let us in. I can explain. Don't tell Zane what happened. Say it was a misunderstanding.

A misunderstanding? What was she thinking? Zane wouldn't believe their belongings sat on the lawn because of a *misunderstanding*.

Zane tugged at Brandy's arm and said, "Why is your back turned? What you hiding?"

Brandy jabbed a finger at his face. She felt stupid and didn't need him nagging her. "Stop touching me. You always assuming something negative. That ain't a good look on you."

She owed him an explanation, but pride wouldn't let her confess. When he shoved her finger away from his face, it made her feel like lying was justified. If he got physical just for suspecting her, what would he do when he learned the truth? Aunt Sheila was upset because Brandy wouldn't allow her to control her. Brandy could smooth things over once she spoke to her aunt, put a few extra dollars in her pocket, and everything would return to normal. Sure, Aunt Sheila would cuss her out for disobeying her, but they would get to sleep in their beds tonight.

Aunt Sheila replied, *Get y'all stuff off my grass, and good luck finding another place to stay. Don't ring my doorbell. Leave my keys in the mailbox.* She sent a peace emoji as if this were a game. This was their life.

It's too late for this. Forgive me. I'm about to Cash App you, Brandy texted while shoving Zane away when he looked over her shoulder.

Rather than show love to her only niece, her aunt said, *Forget you and your Cash App. Get away from my house before I call the cops.*

She underestimated her aunt. There was no reasoning with her. Defeated, she exited the car with Zane on her heels. He barked at her to turn on her camera flashlight because his phone was dead. Brandy stared at Zane while he searched through the bags and boxes. There was no need for her to help him figure out whose belongings they were when she already knew.

"All of this is our stuff. Your aunt is a bitch, but something tells me you know more than you're saying." He stopped rifling through the bags and waited for Brandy to respond, but he wouldn't get an answer that easily. "You ain't got nothing to say?"

Brandy hunched her shoulders.

"Why would she put us out when we paid rent?" she countered. Zane didn't answer, but the furious expression on his face let Brandy know he knew something was off. Then she confessed, "I know why our things are outside. Before you and I went to the club, my aunt said she would put us out if we came home after midnight. She didn't want us to disturb her so-called beauty sleep. But we're grown and pay rent." What twenty-three-year-old woman and twenty-four-year-old man had a curfew? Aunt Sheila had never given them a curfew before.

"She ain't never had a problem with us staying out late." Zane got in her face. "Was she the one blowing up your phone at the club?"

Brandy avoided eye contact because the truth hurt. She'd never been big on taking accountability for her actions. "That was her."

Zane cussed and paced, like he wanted to punch something. Probably her. She stood far from Zane, allowing him space to think and let out his anger. She avoided conflicts with loved ones because someone could get hurt. Since he held a special place in her heart, she didn't want to do anything she'd later regret. She had told him the truth, so that should've ended the conversation.

In the middle of Zane's muttering, his face contorted into a look of rage. He stalked over to Brandy, mushing her forehead as he berated her. "You dumb bitch!" So much for giving him space. He took things too far, but she'd keep calm since she was to blame.

"Your aunt told you she was throwing us out and you didn't care," Zane belted out. "You know I don't have a place to stay, and this is how you treat your best friend. I'm homeless cause of you!" He walked to the porch and dug in his pockets. Zane talked to himself, ignoring Brandy, who joined him on the stairs. "I bet Sheila threw my stuff out because she thought I was ignoring her, too. I can't find my keys." He addressed her, "Unlock the door! You see I need help."

Earlier, when she ignored her aunt's texts and calls, she justified her actions. She and Zane had partied in East Chicago at Zane's associate's house. The liquor, weed, and conversations had been flowing, and Brandy didn't want the night to end. The day before, she had been depressed. Today, she awoke feeling good and had too much energy to sit at home to waste it. Her life stopped when she felt depressed. She isolated herself in her room and failed to check on her four-year-old daughter, Braelynn, who had been in foster care for one year. Though Brandy loved her daughter and desired to reunite with her, she'd had no contact with her child for several weeks. Brandy only had enough energy to eat once a day and use the restroom. Her former boss was to blame for Child Protective Services (CPS) taking Braelynn away, and for Brandy losing her two-bedroom, low-income home. Brandy's former boss had gotten in her face a year ago, threatening to fire her in front of her coworkers. Brandy spat on the woman. Although Brandy had been late to work and had gotten verbal and written warnings, she had deserved respect.

"I forgot my house keys," Brandy lied. "My aunt said to get our stuff and leave. Why are you trying to go inside? Our things are out here." She pointed at their belongings and attempted to scare him when she said, "She threatened to call twelve."

Zane banged on the front door, not caring about the sleeping neighbors. "Open up, Sheila! We need to talk."

Brandy knew he had heard her, but she wouldn't press the matter. If she heard police sirens, she would be out of there, and Zane would be, too. They both had unregistered guns. Zane needed to focus. They had bigger things to worry about, like where they'd stay tonight.

"Let's go," Brandy said. Although she wore a sweater dress, a leather jacket, and knee-high boots, she was cold. Zane ignored her and continued to beat on the door. "We'll get a hotel and figure things out in the morning," she urged.

"I'm not leaving without talking to her. We're saving money to buy a house, and spending money on motels is goofy. If she hears me out, she'll know I wasn't ignoring her. You can stay at a motel, not me."

Before she could protest about how easy it was for him to abandon her, the front porch light turned on and the door opened. Aunt Sheila stood there looking like she was ready to fight, wearing a bonnet and a gown that had seen better days. "Why are y'all banging on my door at this time of morning? What part of, 'y'all stuff would be on the front lawn if you didn't come home by curfew', didn't you two understand?" Not giving either of them time to respond, she continued, "I don't know how many warning texts I sent y'all. You both need a place of your own so you can create your own rules. Y'all been here a year."

Back in the day, Aunt Sheila and Brandy's father lived with their parents until they died. Her aunt pretended like she always had her life together. Brandy would remind her aunt where she came from if she didn't stop talking recklessly.

"Brandy never told me about our new curfew," Zane said.

"I texted you, too, so don't put this all on Brandy."

Aunt Sheila began closing the door when Zane jammed his foot in it and said, "My phone died. Let us move back in, and we'll pay extra this month." Zane sounded pitiful, and he was supposed to be a gangsta.

"I like you, but it won't look right if you stay and she goes. My man wouldn't be okay with that." Aunt Sheila was full of herself. She was old as hell, and no one in their right mind would assume Zane wanted her.

Tired of the back and forth, Brandy pleaded with Zane. "I haven't taken my medication because it makes me dizzy, and I can't think straight. I haven't felt this good in so long. All I wanted was to party with you. My mind kept telling me we should go when it was close to curfew, but I couldn't force myself." Now she sounded pathetic, and the look her aunt gave her solidified it. She was cutting Aunt Sheila off once they left this house. She touched Zane's arm. "You forgive me?"

Zane pulled away from her and addressed Aunt Sheila, "You heard your niece. Can we move back in? We've already paid rent. You know how she gets when she's off her pills." So much for forgiveness.

At least he included Brandy when he mentioned moving back in instead of thinking of only himself. It was a positive sign he was warming back up to her.

"Aunty, let him stay. I messed up. I'll go," she tried again. Brandy's eyes met Zane's, searching for a warm expression, but to no avail.

With her hand on her fat hips, Aunt Sheila said, "I've made my decision. You're my brother's child, and I promised him on his deathbed I'd look out for you, but you're more than I bargained for. One moment you're crying and moping, messing up the energy in my house. The next, you're buying clothes and shoes you don't need, lottery tickets galore, and staying out all night acting like the Energizer Bunny."

Everything she said was true, but Brandy wasn't entirely to blame for her mental health issues. When she was in elementary school, a psychiatrist diagnosed her father with Bipolar I during one of his many psychiatric ward stays. Over the years, he would remain stable for a period, only to return to an erratic state. When off his medication, her father cussed people out, fought, and once stripped in a grocery store because the owner wouldn't give him a discount on a rib-eye steak.

Anytime Brandy blamed genetics, she felt guilty, because she really did love her father. But it was true; his genes sucked. Brandy didn't have a fair start in life. People referred to her now-deceased mother as crazy, though no doctor had ever diagnosed her with a mental illness. Her mother used to fight and cuss. Despite her parents' violent histories, they never became physical with one another, although they argued occasionally.

Brandy's mother took it in stride when Brandy's father had manic episodes and wouldn't come home for days. Her father knew how bad his condition could get, so when he was stable, he gave Brandy's mother extra money to save so she could pay the bills when he disappeared during his next manic stage. When money got short, Brandy's mother relied on her illegal hustle, using her good looks to set up drug dealers.

When Brandy was seventeen, someone discovered her mother's body in an alley. That devastated Brandy because she and her mother had been close. What made matters worse was that they never found the killer. There were no witnesses, and that traumatized Brandy as much as her mother's death. After burying her mother, Brandy's moods were up and down. One moment she was depressed and locked herself in her bedroom. Next, she stayed out from noon to early the following morning sleeping with more boys than she had in the past, before advancing to having sex with older men.

Aunt Sheila visited the home Brandy shared with her father one day, and her aunt found drawers of scratched-off lottery tickets and clothes Brandy had stolen. When her aunt asked about it, Brandy spoke so fast her aunt couldn't keep up. That was when her aunt scheduled her for an appointment with a psychiatrist who prescribed psychotropic medication. It took several types of pills to find ones that worked for Brandy. Like her father, she had trouble taking her medication consistently. Getting diagnosed with Bipolar II increased her compassion for her father. Once she entered a hypomanic state, she never wanted to come down from the high she felt. The medication mellowed her.

Not long after Brandy's mother passed, doctors diagnosed Brandy's father with pancreatic cancer, and he died two years later. Unfortunately, her father didn't take his bipolar medication consistently until after he got cancer. By that time, he was so sick that Brandy couldn't enjoy being around him or make up for the time they lost when she was younger.

"I'll be expecting my rent back sooner rather than later." Zane pointed a finger at Aunt Sheila; his confidence returned.

After Aunt Sheila nodded and closed the door, Zane placed his belongings in Brandy's trunk, not leaving much room for her things. Instead of complaining, she left whatever couldn't fit in the back seat on the lawn for anyone who wanted the items.

Neither Zane nor Brandy had furniture, which was embarrassing. Brandy lost hers after getting evicted, and Zane left his at the home he once shared with his baby mama, Sherita, who ultimately threw him out of his own apartment.

Had it not been for having money in the bank, Brandy would've gotten down on herself. At least she had a car. Zane gave his car to Sherita to ensure their kids got back and forth to school. Sherita made a ridiculous mistake by not forgiving Zane. Although he was a video game addict, he loved his kids and Sherita.

Once Brandy drove off, she said, "I'm so—"

"I don't want to hear it. We had one goal: save money to buy a house for our kids. You ruined that. I wonder if you even care about Braelynn being in foster care. You may not care about her, but I do. I want my sons to live with me. Once I show Sherita I own a home, she might let them live with me. If not, I'll take her ass to court for equal custody."

Brandy stewed in her seat. Zane had a right to be angry, but he didn't have to be disrespectful. "Don't bring up my baby. I love her more than anything in this world. We'll get a house for our kids and the courts will see I'm a good parent. It's going to take a little longer than expected."

"A delay in buying a house is unacceptable, since you could've avoided it," Zane said. "I need a blunt." They had money saved, so Zane was overreacting. The hotels would eat up some of their funds, but that only meant they'd have to do illegal things to balance everything out.

No matter how hard she tried, Brandy couldn't stop thinking about Zane's criticism of her as a mother. She wasn't sensitive, but anything to do with her daughter was sensitive. After Brandy's boss fired her last year, she fell into depression and stopped caring for her daughter. Then CPS got involved. The judge should've been lenient considering Brandy's mental condition. A few neighbors chastised her for allowing Braelynn to sit on the porch alone. Not that Brandy allowed it. Braelynn would unlock the door and go outside when she couldn't wake Brandy. It hadn't been her proudest moment. While depressed, she saw nothing wrong with her daughter eating a meal a day, and Brandy combing her hair occasionally. Zane had been a tremendous help during that time, often taking Braelynn to stay at his apartment with his family. But he couldn't keep her all the time.

The court ordered Brandy bi-weekly supervised visits, but she'd missed the last few because of depression. Braelynn would be better off without her. Her daughter's foster parents were decent people, and Braelynn looked happy. Brandy wished she could get Zane's thoughts on whether she should allow the foster parents to adopt her child. But she couldn't. He'd judge her. Since Braelynn had been in foster care, things changed between Brandy and Zane. They still spent time together when she was in a good mood; however, Zane stopped confiding in her and no longer held her when she couldn't leave her bed. He resented her but wouldn't admit it. But his sarcasm and criticism spoke volumes.

Feeling herself start to spiral, Brandy told herself to stop worrying about it. She could still fix this. She devised a scheme to improve Zane's and her life.

Zane blurted his idea before she could share hers. "I know what we need to do. You won't want to do it, but you owe me."

"I'll do anything."

He divulged his most treacherous scheme ever. Had their night gone differently, Brandy would've declined, but she felt indebted to him. He had made a good point. They had to pay for the motel. Why use their money when they could use someone else's?

2

BRANDY

ZANE HAD DONE SHEISTY things in the past, but this was an all-time low. Normally, Brandy was down to rob. She'd done it many times, but she didn't rob people she knew and liked. Not long after leaving her aunt's, they pulled up to the alley behind Ms. Robinson's house. Ms. Robinson, Sherita's mother, had always been nice to Brandy, who often saw her when Zane and Sherita dated. Zane despised Ms. Robinson, whom he blamed for ending his relationship with her daughter.

Sherita kicked him out when she discovered he lied about being out of the streets. For a while, she believed him because he got a legit gig delivering food and groceries and transporting passengers. But he had one foot in the streets and one foot out. Zane got exposed when an unknown person messaged Sherita online telling her the truth. Sherita hesitated to believe the stranger until her mother convinced her it had to be true. Zane often bought gym shoes and clothes. Since he spent more money than a typical gig worker, it was likely he was involved in illegal activities.

After it became clear Sherita wouldn't take him back, Zane continued begging her to forgive him. Vitiligo and his short height made Zane overcompensate. Brandy thought he was handsome. He stood at five feet seven inches. Brandy didn't judge others for being short since she was four feet nine. In school, people teased her for being short with huge breasts. The teasing never failed to confuse her. Her height and triple-D breasts were not her choice. Although Zane wouldn't admit it, vitiligo caused him to have low self-esteem, too. He never pursued gorgeous women, only the ones most men overlooked, and he never took pictures. Before his sons were born, he confessed to Brandy that he often prayed they wouldn't get vitiligo, so other children wouldn't bully them. Whenever Brandy encouraged him about his looks, he dismissed her. She wished he'd see himself how she saw him.

Before exiting the car, they surveyed their surroundings. Everything was clear, so they put on their gloves and masks. Outside, Brandy grabbed Ms. Robinson's garbage container and followed Zane to the dining room window, where he used the barrel of his gun to break the window. They used the garbage container to boost themselves into the same dining room where Brandy had enjoyed Ms. Robinson's soul food. If everything went smoothly, Brandy would make a plate of food before leaving. Ms. Robinson always cooked more food than she could've eaten.

There was no reason this wouldn't be a straightforward job. They had guns, but Brandy didn't plan to use hers. Hopefully, Zane felt the same. If Ms. Robinson caught them, how embarrassing would that be? She would tell everyone, including Aunt Sheila. Aunt Sheila would feel validated. Sherita wouldn't allow Zane to see their children. As Brandy followed Zane through the house, she felt bad about what they were doing but convinced herself she and Zane needed money more than Ms. Robinson. When they passed Ms. Robinson's closed bedroom door, Brandy heard the woman snoring. Zane was certain Ms. Robinson was the only one in the home; she was single and never talked about men. They crept to the spare bedroom, and Zane rummaged through shoe boxes in the closet. According to him, Ms. Robinson didn't trust banks, so she kept her money stored in shoe boxes.

"Hurry," Brandy whispered because Zane was noisy. He threw boxes of shoes onto the floor and hadn't discovered one dollar. If he was wrong about the money, that would upset Brandy. She robbed a house dressed in party clothes when she could've been at the motel asleep. Too bad she hadn't thought to ask Zane earlier if he'd seen Ms. Robinson store money in this room. If Ms. Robinson were smart, she would have hidden the money in shoe boxes in her bedroom. If they had to go into her room, so be it. Brandy refused to leave empty-handed.

"Focus on your job. That old bitch got money in this closet. I saw Sherita take money from a box when she thought I was asleep."

Brandy overreacted and needed to calm down. She could hear Ms. Robinson still snoring. Zane opened another shoe box and waved money at Brandy. He stuck out his tongue at her, and she gave him the finger. It was about time. They could leave.

After Zane left the room, she followed. To her surprise, Ms. Robinson's door opened. Brandy couldn't fathom shooting Ms. Robinson unless the old woman attacked them. Brandy darted behind Zane so Ms. Robinson wouldn't see her outfit. If Ms. Robinson saw that one robber was a female, she might've realized it was them.

"What the h—" said Ms. Robinson, who stepped into the hallway.

Zane hit Ms. Robinson in the head with his gun and knocked her to the ground, where she lay unconscious, dressed in a robe. What Zane did was wrong, but he had no choice. His putting Ms. Robinson to sleep was better than shooting her. Ms. Robinson might agree.

They trashed the living room and dining room to make it look like a robbery. Before leaving, Brandy glanced at Ms. Robinson, who remained asleep.

***

Brandy drove while Zane counted the money.

"Five hundred and fifty dollars will buy us a few nights at a motel." They'd have to rob again, and soon. If they did it too frequently, they'd end up in jail, or worse: dead. Brandy had to think of a better solution. "If that old bitch would've minded her business, I wouldn't have done her like that," Zane said. He wasn't the least bit concerned about the old woman, despite her being his children's grandmother.

"I hope Ms. Robinson is okay. We should've robbed someone else." Guilt had gotten the better of Brandy. Who knew how long it would take for her to bounce back from her injury? Brandy looked over at Zane, who showed no glimmer of compassion.

"Don't start," Zane said, putting the money away. "You didn't have a better idea. I shouldn't always have to save us. When are you going to have our backs? The doctor gave you those pills for you to take, not use as decoration."

"You were living with me and my aunt, so what do you mean I never have your back? And you don't know how those pills make me feel—"

"I don't care about the side effects. When you take them, you act like a grown-ass woman instead of a kid. I paid rent to stay with your aunt and paid part of yours when you refused to work. You're welcome."

When angry, Zane was heartless. He was nothing like the cowardly boy he once was when he transferred to Brandy's middle school. She was the only person who befriended him after collaborating with him on a science project that they both failed. The popular boys made fun of Zane for having vitiligo. Zane never stood up for himself.

Brandy was a loner in middle school. The girls didn't like her because she tried taking their men to prove she wasn't ugly. A few of the boys slept with her and then called her names as if they didn't engage in the act with her. Had it not been for Brandy helping Zane with his confidence, he'd still be inside his shell. But he never gave her credit for how she looked out for him over the years. Whenever she brought it up, he reminded her that in high school, people called him 'The Knock-Out King' because he knocked out boys who disrespected her. He and Brandy remained close because Zane said he could trust her more than boys his age. They even dropped out together in the eleventh grade. Why keep going to school if all they got were Ds and Fs?

Zane turned on the car radio and blasted it to ignore her. She drove to the nearest motel, feeling misunderstood and undervalued.

3

BRANDY

THE NEXT MORNING, ZANE seemed less annoyed with Brandy as she watched him play a video game in bed before he prepared for work. While Zane excelled at robbing anyone he caught lacking, he also took on gig work to earn the necessary pay stubs for their future home. Since they only had one car, Zane worked mornings and late afternoons, while Brandy delivered food late evenings.

Even though Brandy hadn't slept, she wasn't tired. During manic episodes, it was hard to sleep. Zane was the opposite. He could fall asleep easily and sleep through an earthquake if they had those in Gary, Indiana. When depressed, all Brandy did was sleep, so what a relief it had been to have energy. Once Zane left, she'd see what there was to do within walking distance of the motel.

Finished playing his game, Zane stood in the mirror, brushing his hair. Brandy noticed him looking at her like he had something to say. Finally, he said, "I'm about to FaceTime Braelynn. I'll put you on with her and the foster parents when I'm done." After Brandy rolled her eyes, he continued, "What the hell is wrong with you? When you were depressed, I understood why you didn't talk to her or visit her, but you're feeling better now."

Her depression had only just lifted yesterday. From the way he talked, one could assume she had been in a much better mood for several weeks.

Why did he feel the need to judge? Whether it was Zane or her aunt or the judge, they all reminded her she was an unfit mother. Even the foster parents gave her questionable looks when they thought she wasn't looking.

"I'm wearing a nightgown. I don't want to be on camera."

Brandy couldn't care less about what she wore—but she was ashamed it had been weeks since she'd spoken to her child. Who knew if Braelynn wanted to talk to her? Her daughter was young, but kids could sense when their parents weren't that into them. When Zane grunted, Brandy felt bad, so she reminded herself that she was a good enough mother. Eventually, she'd talk to her daughter, but not today. She had to work up her confidence.

"At least Braelynn has me looking after her. She misses you, though. You need to do better."

His words were like a sharp machete lashing away at her heart and the little self-respect she had left. Although Zane was right, she didn't want to hear it.

"Back off. I'm working with you to buy a house, so that makes me a damn good mother. She's too young to know why she lives with foster parents."

"Stop lying to yourself."

Before she could think of a sarcastic comeback, Zane jumped on the call with Braelynn, and tears ran down Brandy's face at the sound of her voice. Thoughts of neglecting her child took over her mind. Before she was taken, her daughter would cry and tap her on the shoulder, letting her know she wanted food and water, only to be ignored. Back then, Brandy wanted to get out of bed, but it felt like shackles weighed her down. All she could think about was missing her parents and asking God why her life took a turn for the worse. Her mother would never know she had a grandchild. During a hypomanic episode, Brandy got pregnant. She avoided thinking about Braelynn's father because she never told him the baby was his. She blamed herself for getting pregnant.

It became overwhelming listening to Zane talk to Braelynn and the foster parents, so Brandy went to the car until Zane left for work. She rejoiced that he was gone. She didn't need him bringing her down, reminding her of the failure she was. Once dressed, she styled her shoulder-length hair in curls and applied makeup, careful to contour her nose to reduce its size because kids used to say she had a bell pepper-shaped nose.

She played pop music and let it blast through her phone speakers. Soon, she forgot about her troubles. She jumped on the bed like a child and sang at the top of her lungs like she was on stage with Taylor Swift. She could be herself now that Zane was gone. He gave her a hard time for liking pop music. Homelessness wasn't as bad as she had imagined. The knock on the door ended her one-person party.

Through the peephole, she saw a man wearing a shirt with the motel's name and logo.

The worker said, "Can you turn down the music?" Brandy didn't appreciate the upset look on the man's face or his tone. She'd go off if he didn't correct his attitude. But for now, she humbled herself by smiling and cracking the door. Her smile had no impact on the worker's demeanor. "We've received several complaints about loud music. I ask that you respect our other guests and keep it down."

Who did he think he was talking to? She closed the door in his face. He'd knocked too loudly for a person who should've been professional. After she turned down the music, she returned to the door with an attitude. "I paid my money like everybody else, and I have the right to enjoy my stay. Who snitched?" She stuck her head out the door and looked down the hall as if a person wearing an 'I Snitched' t-shirt would walk past her.

Frustrated, the worker said, "I'm not at liberty to share with you who called the front desk. Just keep your music down." He had gone into the wrong field. Customer service wasn't for him.

Brandy had had enough. She shut the door. Being told what to do was the absolute worst. She let others live their lives on their terms and wished people would grant her the same courtesy. To avoid getting thrown out, she kept the music down, but that didn't stop her from dancing around the room as if she were at a concert.

Minutes later, she freshened her makeup since she had danced so hard she worked up a sweat. She looked too good to stay in the room. The other guests had to lay eyes on her. Why do your makeup and hair if no one saw you? She left the room and walked through the halls of the motel.

Two women looked her over and snickered when they passed her, and one said to the other, "Why does she have on so much makeup?"

Brandy couldn't ignore the comment. "Hoe Number One and Hoe Number Two, y'all want to get drug down this hall?" She could take both of them with no problems. No woman had ever beaten Brandy in a fight, and she wouldn't lose her winning streak today. Fortunately for the women, Brandy had forgotten her gun in the room. She would have waved it around to frighten them. If the hoes wanted help with their makeup, all they had to do was ask. Women were haters. That was why she didn't have female friends.

The woman who commented on Brandy's makeup grabbed her friend's arm and they got out of there. Cowards.

"That's what I thought," Brandy said. For fun, she ran after them. When they noticed her following, they screamed and ran. Once they turned the corner, Brandy stopped chasing them. She wouldn't have done anything. Their reaction made her feel powerful.

Seconds later, Brandy strolled down another hallway. She craved sex and desired to catch the eye of a trick. Not long after, she made eye contact with an older man and licked her thick lips, which made him come to her. He wore jean shorts, a Hawaiian shirt, and brown sandals. His clothing told the world that he'd retire in Florida soon. Though not her type, he'd do. The man smiled as he looked down at her, his eyes lingering on her breasts. She hadn't had sex in weeks, and she and Zane needed more money for his dream house. If she could show Zane her ability to make money without him, he'd see she didn't solely depend on him.

When she noticed the man's wedding ring, he shoved his hand in his pocket as if she cared. She didn't, and almost told him that, but wanted to give off the impression she was a lady.

"My wife and I separated. I should stop wearing the ring, but old habits die hard. I'm Marvin." He looked over his shoulders like he was looking for someone, perhaps his wife.

"Sorry things didn't work out with your wife," she lied. To stop Marvin's wife or kids from walking up on them, Brandy moved things along. "I'm bored. You want to come to my room and listen to music?" She rubbed his chest to signal what she wanted in case he was slow.

She'd learned that a sensual touch could get her nearly anything—including sex. Marvin's lustful expression showed he was going to fall for her. He stroked Brandy's arm, still resting on his chest, and grinned. He didn't bother to ask her name or what kind of music they'd listen to. His attire told her he was a fan of old-school R&B and hated any up-to-date music.

Before she could bring up the subject of money, Marvin opened his wallet, pulled out several bills, and winked. He said, "This should be enough."

Brandy had mixed feelings when Marvin brought up money. It pleased her because she despised bargaining money for sex. That was never easy, despite how many times she'd done it before. It offended her because he assumed she was a prostitute. She glanced at her size fourteen, long jean skirt with the split up the front that revealed her chunky thighs. Her sweater was a perfect fit, emphasizing her waist and breasts. There was nothing about her outfit that suggested she was a hoe. If she didn't fear sounding insecure, she would've asked how he knew she was selling pussy.

Back in the room, Brandy played rock music to set the mood and ignored the concerned look on Marvin's face. His dislike for her taste in music vanished when she stripped; his eyes fixated on her breasts. Her eyes lit up when Marvin's dick swelled. Maybe she'd get some pleasure out of this. The money was the goal, but if he could make her feel good, that was a bonus. He undressed and lay on the bed, eager to be pleased. Brandy joined him.

During sex, it became apparent he couldn't please her. But to give him his money's worth, she screamed as loud as she could and made the head-board slam against the wall. From Marvin's grunts and the jerking of his body, he'd go down in history as a happy client.

Marvin dressed and rifled through his wallet. "I'm sorry, mama," he said, "I forgot I had to pay to stay here tonight, so I'm forty dollars short." He avoided eye contact. Shameless, he tapped her on the shoulder. "Thanks for the fun time. My wife is older and doesn't give me the same experience she did when she was younger. I like young girls like yourself who can keep up with my energy." He tossed money on the bed as if she were a cheap hoe.

What happened to his separation? Not that it mattered. All men were liars, but he had gotten too comfortable with her. He no longer cared about her feelings, and he tried to finesse her. Brandy hated his type. His poor wife likely sat in their motel room thinking her husband loved her, but here Marvin stood, cheating and speaking recklessly about her.

"A fun time requires good pay. We had an agreement." Brandy got out of the bed and dressed in case she had to run after Marvin. "I'd hate to find your wife and tell her you paid me to have sex with my gay friend without a condom. Does she know you prefer the bottom?"

They used a condom, but that wasn't what she'd tell his wife. She wouldn't rest until she got all her money. Any lie she could think of to ruin his happy life would come out of her mouth. He'd better stop playing. As if something were funny, Marvin laughed. That wasn't the response she'd expected.

"My wife won't believe I had sex with you. You look like a clown with all that makeup. My wife is a reserved, God-fearing woman." With a look of disgust, he pointed at Brandy. "You, my dear, look crazy, but I like crazy. You all give the best—" He put his thumb in his mouth, sucked it, and moaned. Done mocking her, he approached the door to leave.

Did she have too much makeup on? The women in the hall laughed and said the same thing. Earlier, when Brandy looked in the mirror, she looked fine. She racked her brain, thinking of a time she had ever been this disrespected. Although she didn't know him and charged him for sex, that didn't give him the right to treat her like she was beneath him and his wife. Sleeping with men for money didn't make her a bad person. She had nothing to be ashamed of. Every time she opened her legs to them, men should compensate her.

In Marvin's younger years, he wouldn't have wanted to be seen with a woman like Brandy in the daytime. Only attractively challenged men would enjoy having her on their arms while the sun shone.

Brandy preferred to get her money the easy way, so she used charm rather than cuss him out. "Come here, Daddy." When he faced her, she ran her hands through her hair and motioned for him to sit in the chair by the door. She pointed between his legs. "Let me massage it once more and you can keep the forty dollars."

Like the goofy he was, he obeyed. Some men thought too much of themselves. He assumed the tables had turned, and he was now doing her a favor. Unzipping his pants, he said, "The way you were moaning told me I satisfied you. You want more of Daddy, huh? Bring your chitlins and hog maw eating behind here."

Had this not been serious, she would've laughed in the old nigga's face. She'd never had chitlins, and the latter thing he mentioned didn't register in her mind. If Zane knew what Brandy had planned for Marvin, he'd accuse her of 'over whoopin,' or overreacting. She wasn't doing too much. Marvin deserved what he was about to get. "Let me grab a condom." Brandy opened the drawer, grabbed her gun, and pointed it at Marvin. The surprise on his face showed he sensed the power dynamics had changed. "Are you done whoopin'?"

The once confident Marvin stuttered, "W-whoopin'? W-what does that mean?" She stayed silent. "You don't have to do this. I have a family, and they'll be looking for me." He reached behind him for his wallet.

"I didn't tell you to move. Listen, or you won't make it out of here alive. Stand, put your hands up, and jump on one leg."

Marvin hesitated.

"Remember, I'm crazy, and I come from a long line of crazy people. If I shoot you, I'll end up in a mental hospital and get out soon because you raped me after I invited you to listen to music."

"Rape? They won't believe you. Look at me and look at you." Although he jumped on one leg with his hands in the air, the arrogance resurfaced. Brandy had run out of options. She could shoot him, but she'd end up in prison. He wasn't worth it.

"Rape! Rape! Rape!" Brandy screamed. "No, no, Marvin, I don't want to have sex with you. Help! He's trying to rape me." If the neighbors on either side of her room had been in their rooms when Brandy and Marvin had sex earlier, they'd say they heard her begging him to do all kinds of nasty things to her body. She'd say she consented the first time but refused the second, and then he raped her.

"Shut up!" He stepped toward her with a finger over his mouth, attempting to quiet her. "Tell me what you want. I'll do anything."

His telling her to shut up meant she hadn't humbled him enough. She'd teach him. "No!" she called out. "I don't want to have sex with you again. I won't do it, Marvin. Please stop grabbing me, Marvin!"

Marvin's uncoordinated ass stumbled and grabbed the end table to break his fall. "May I get my wallet so I can pay you and get the hell out of here?"

"Apologize while you slowly take out your wallet." Brandy faked crying with the gun trained on Marvin. "You hurt my feelings when you called me ugly. Ain't I beautiful?"

"Whatever you say, ma'am." Marvin grabbed his wallet in slow motion and put forty dollars on the end table. "You're the most beautiful woman in the world." His sarcastic tone proved unsatisfying to her.

"Say it like you mean it or I'll send you to Jesus." She was bluffing, but he didn't know it.

"Baby, you're the most beautiful woman I've laid eyes on." Marvin was quite the actor when he wanted to be. If she didn't know any better, she'd believe him.

"Thank you, sir. Now leave all your money and get the fuck out."

"My wife will wonder what happened to our money. I can't do that."

After Brandy pointed the gun at his head, he set down all his money, including coins. "May I go?" he asked.

She waved him off, and he left. Brandy stuck her head out the door. "Let's do it again tomorrow. Same time. Same place." He didn't respond.

She counted the money. Altogether, she got four hundred dollars and some change. This might make Zane proud, but she was uncertain. These days he was hard to please.

To celebrate, she cranked up the music while she washed the remnants of Marvin off her body. The beating at the door prevented her from drying off properly. After getting dressed, she peeked out the peephole at the rude motel worker and Marvin. Marvin was a snitch. How would she get out of this?

After cracking the door, Brandy asked the worker what he wanted, and he demanded to talk to her face-to-face, so she opened the door.

Marvin said to the worker, "That's the hoe that stole my money. All I want is my money, and I'll be on my way."

"Lies," said Brandy. "I don't have his money." She turned to the worker. "Are we done?"

With too much bass in his voice, the worker said, "Prostitution is prohibited. Miss, you need to leave. Before receiving the prostitution complaint, neighbors complained. One about loud sex. Another reported loud music. I knocked five minutes before you answered."

When Marvin smirked, Brandy had a strong urge to hit him with her gun. She had to keep her composure to avoid getting put out. It would look irresponsible, and Zane would go off.

"Why are you threatening to put me out? I'll turn down my music. Marvin is lying."

"I'm not going back and forth with her. Tell her to give me my money," said Marvin, who hit her door with his fist.

The worker addressed Marvin, "Calm down. Call the police if she has your money because she denied it. It's not in my job scope to oversee these kinds of disputes. You need to leave the motel, too."

While Marvin and the worker argued about fairness and motel policies, Brandy interrupted and said to the worker, "Marvin should leave, not me! You know what? Let me speak to your manager."

The worker pointed at himself. "I'm the manager, and my word is final. You and he have half an hour to pack and leave, or I'm calling the police to report trespassing and prostitution. This is a decent place, not a hole in the wall meant for forty-dollar blow jobs."

Both Brandy and Marvin cussed at the manager who dismissed them by walking off. The motel owner should fire him.

"Head wasn't forty dollars, it was sixty!" Brandy yelled at him as he kept his back to her while walking away. "Show me respect."

Another motel guest covered his young daughter's ears as they approached Brandy's door. The man scowled at Brandy and Marvin. His judgment meant nothing to Brandy because once he got his daughter in the room, he'd come back later knocking at Brandy's door for the sixty-dollar blow job.

"Your big crybaby ass," she said to Marvin. "You couldn't leave our problem between us?" Before he could respond, Brandy shoved him, slammed the door in his face, and disregarded his knocks and rants. Why had he snitched? The man had no shame. What did he think would happen after confessing to tricking at the motel?

She should've contacted Zane but didn't want to disturb him at work. Honestly, she didn't want to explain what had happened at all. She packed their belongings, and soon after, she stood at the front desk with the motel worker.

Given time to consider the weight of getting put out of two places in such a brief period, Brandy said to the worker, "Hear me out. Give me another chance and you won't hear another complaint. I need this place. If you don't help me, you'll be ending a lifelong friendship." Not only would Zane blame her if they had to leave, but this might break their bond. How much more could he take? Zane would think she was the biggest idiot walking, and she couldn't have that.

The worker picked up the motel phone and dialed. "I need the police at—"

Brandy left. She pulled her and Zane's belongings to the sidewalk and made a few trips from the motel to the bus stop on the corner. It was risky, but she stored their things there. She'd sit on the bus bench waiting for Zane to ride past.

Moments later, Marvin and a woman Brandy assumed to be his wife pulled up to the bus stop. The passenger's side window rolled down, and the woman screamed, "Greedy hoe! I should whoop your ugly—"

Lifting her shirt, Brandy exposed her gun. "I got it on me. Step out of the car."

Before the car pulled off, Marvin and the woman gave Brandy the finger. His wife didn't seem like a church-going woman, not with that language and making threats. She was older and pretty, but Brandy's youth triumphed, making what that woman said irrelevant. Brandy had bigger things to consider, like where she and Zane would stay tonight. She had no friends besides him; Facebook friends didn't count. Zane had associates, but none who would give him a place to stay. In times like this, she wished she and Zane had other close friends they could rely on, but neither liked people.

With time to think, she produced an idea. She knew where they could stay rent-free. Zane wouldn't like it because it would be unlike anything they'd ever done, but it would beat homelessness. She had worked as a food delivery driver for nearly a year. She liked the job because she created her own schedule, and the flexibility allowed her to miss work when depressed.

Although she wasn't well acquainted with her clients, she knew some of their habits. One woman had cheated on her husband. Brandy knew this because most times when Brandy dropped off groceries at the client's house, the client pushed a man out the door, telling him to hurry and leave before he got them both killed. Another client had agoraphobia. When Brandy dropped off groceries, she didn't come to the door. She held off and waited for Brandy to get in the car before grabbing her delivery from the porch. Her door was never fully open; she only cracked it to grab her deliveries with her arm. Brandy had never seen the woman's face. That client was the perfect prey. Based on Brandy's observations, the client appeared to be living alone. No cars were ever parked in front of the house. The client seemed unloved, since she was alone on a dead-end street. She probably had an aversion to being around people or having phone conversations. Nobody would unexpectedly show up at her home.

For Brandy's plan to work, all she and Zane had to do was take the woman hostage in her home and stack their money. The only issue was whether Zane would go along with it. It sounded crazy, but she doubted he'd have a better option. How would they ensure the client didn't snitch once they moved out of her home? He could help her brainstorm. They could kill the woman, but Brandy had never taken a life, and neither had he. She disregarded the thought. Brandy and Zane weren't murderers. It was possible Zane might kill Brandy once he realized she'd gotten them tossed out—again.

4

BRANDY

Hours passed while Brandy waited at the bus stop. Annoyed bus drivers sped off after discovering she wasn't waiting for a bus. It was their job to serve, but like the motel worker, the bus drivers behaved as if she had somehow imposed upon them. When she wasn't people-watching, she scrolled on her phone and contemplated calling Zane to tell him they got kicked out, but never worked up the courage.

When she spotted him driving to the motel, she left their belongings at the bus stop to meet him in the parking lot. A part of her wanted to run in the opposite direction. Last night, she held herself back from hitting him when he put his hands on her. Who knew how far he'd take things now? Hopefully, he'd show compassion. If he hit her, she didn't know what she'd do. Brandy loved him, but she wouldn't allow him to beat her up in public and not protect herself. She had a reputation to think of.

Smiling, Zane exited the car. He must've made plenty of tips, which put him in a good mood. "Where are you coming from?" he asked.

She might as well spit it out rather than have Zane go to their room and find out the key didn't work. "We got kicked out of the motel. The funky front desk worker doesn't like me." Watching how quickly Zane's facial expression changed, Brandy talked faster to make him hear her. "I tried explaining to his unprofessional ass that—"

"I don't know who's dumber, me or you?" He could've at least let her finish her sentence.

"You go out of your way to mess up a good thing for yourself and everyone around you! We're done." He walked toward the motel.

Zane made her feel worse. Anything could've happened to her in his absence. She ran after Zane to fight for their friendship. He had to hear her out.

"You don't mean that. If you knew what happened, you wouldn't be mad." He waved her off. She wasted energy but refused to give up. "I have an idea." Stubbornly, he ignored her. "Why are you going to the motel?"

"I'm going to get my shit. Why else would I go inside?"

"Our things are at the bus stop."

An angry laugh escaped him. "This bitch. You left my clothes and games at a damn bus stop? Something is wrong with you." He laughed. Brandy knew him well. He did it to stall so he could think of something disrespectful to say. She braced herself. "It's better you ain't in Braelynn's life. You can't take care of yourself. The system done messed up a lot of Black families, but this time, they got it right. I hope you never get her back. Where is the bus—"

The slap that Brandy gave Zane would make him think twice before speaking to her like that again. His words hurt, but she wouldn't let him know it. He'd made comments about Braelynn before, but today he was beyond cruel, friend or not. Who did he think he was? It's not like he was the father of the year. When dealing with Sherita, he was messier than a scorned woman. Brandy couldn't deny Zane was a better parent than her, but she'd keep that to herself. He'd swell with pride and have more to throw in her face.

One moment she held her head high, feeling accomplished about standing up to Zane. Next, she was on the ground with Zane's finger in her face. Whatever he screamed in her face went in one ear and out the other. Winning a fight against "The Knockout King" was impossible, but she had to prove she wouldn't go down easily. Zane sat on top of Brandy. Grabbing his waist, she threw his thin body off her. The situation didn't play out as she had imagined.

Brandy had assumed she'd get in a few punches. Instead, she didn't let off a single punch before he was back on top of her yelling while spit flew in her face. A crowd formed on the sidewalk, and a woman who looked Brandy's age recorded them. Brandy tried lifting her head to cuss at the woman, but couldn't because Zane overpowered her. He couldn't care less if someone had their phone out.

Two men pulled Zane off her and threw him against the motel building. Relieved, Brandy stood and watched Zane struggle with them. She was glad for the help, but hated seeing Zane lose. He treated her terribly, but friends fight sometimes. What happened was partly her fault. Considering Zane's point of view, she could see why he might believe she was undermining his dream of purchasing a house for them and their children.

Not caring about the consequences, Brandy jumped on the back of the smallest of the two men, which allowed Zane to get loose. With one punch, Zane dropped the guy who, a second ago, had brought Zane to his knees. Next, Zane gave an uppercut to the other man, who struggled to get Brandy off his back. Helping him would mend their relationship. Brandy was sure of it.

More bystanders recorded the scene, but no one intervened. The motel worker threatened to call the police, which ended the fight. Brandy grabbed her purse, which luckily no one had stolen—her gun and money were inside. She and Zane walked to the car, cussing out the two men who walked in the opposite direction.

They drove to the bus stop in silence. She didn't speak because she was in pain from Zane slamming her to the ground. Staring at Zane, Brandy couldn't stop thinking about how easy it was for him to end their friendship. Didn't he love her? The man whose back she jumped on at the motel had been gentler with her than Zane, and that man didn't know her. He was huge and could've slammed her into the wall or thrown her onto the concrete, but he didn't. What did that say about Zane's true feelings for her? Why had he roughly handled her? A part of her blamed herself. Had she had other friends, she could have asked their opinion of who was right or wrong.

Despite everything, she needed him. He was all she had. How many losses could one person take? Her parents died young, Aunt Sheila was insensitive, and Braelynn was in foster care.

Brandy humbled herself. "I'm sorry."

There was no response from Zane. Fine, forget him. If he wanted to be unforgiving, that was on him. When Zane pulled in front of the bus stop, Brandy's mouth dropped. All their things were gone.

Zane said, "Where is our shit?"

Brandy gasped in shock. "Someone took our stuff. What the hell!"

Was she cursed? Why did terrible things keep happening to her? Brandy was a good person. It was as if God wanted her in a mental institution. Brandy had never been to jail, but she suspected today would be the day. Zane went crazy at the motel; what would he do to her now? She should've gotten out of her car and run. Being trapped in a closed space while someone rained blows on her didn't seem wise. Yet, neither was leaving Zane with her car.

Rather than fight or scream, Zane sped off, cut the car off to the left of them, and ran the red light. As several people laid on their horns, Brandy kept her eyes trained on Zane, who refused to make eye contact. He blasted a song on his phone and drove without telling her where they were going. She stared out the passenger's side window, fighting back tears. The only things they had to their names were the clothes on their back, money, and guns. Zane never left home without his gun, even when he went to work.

***

Not long after, Zane parked on the street where Sherita lived and exited the car without a word to Brandy. Why were they there? Would he ditch Brandy if Sherita took him back? Sherita wouldn't allow him to move back in. He wasted his time. Brandy had nothing to worry about.

At the passenger side window, Zane said to Brandy, 'I can't deal with your up-and-down moods. I don't never know what I'm gon' get—depressed you, or crazy you. Fighting for my family is the only thing that makes sense. A nigga ain't hotel hopping or living in your car with you. Because of you, I'm homeless."

Brandy hadn't shared her plan about her agoraphobic client yet. Zane needed time with his thoughts before he could listen. Had she known he was driving to Sherita's, she would've spoken up, so he'd know they had options. Now was the time to tell him so they could leave, but before she could say anything, Sherita came out of the house with the boys: Zane Jr., six, and Deondre, age four. The boys hugged Zane. The smiles on the boys' faces made Brandy wish she were a kid again. As a child, she never had to worry about money or where she'd lay her head at night.

Zane's boys begged him to cut their hair while Sherita stood on the porch, scowling. This was what Zane deserved for popping up unannounced. He knew how Sherita was. Sure enough, she reminded him not to come to her house without calling. Brandy felt bad when Sherita told Zane someone had broken into her mother's house and attacked Ms. Robinson. There were no suspects. Sherita and the boys had been at the hospital most of the day. Ms. Robinson had a knot on her head but was recovering well, so hospital staff would release her later that day. Zane pretended to be shocked, but he really didn't care. Brandy wished Ms. Robinson a speedy recovery.

Sherita ignored Brandy when she saw her sitting in the car. Brandy had helped Zane move after Sherita kicked him out—which, of course, didn't sit well with Sherita. But what did she expect Brandy to do? Let Zane blow money on a moving truck? Brandy stayed in her lane today. She was too drained to argue or fight.

Although Brandy didn't want to get involved, it was hard because Zane embarrassed himself. He grabbed Sherita as if she were the answer to his prayers and ignored her pleas to let her go. Had living with Brandy been that bad? Zane begged Sherita to allow him to move back in and told her Brandy was a screw-up. It blew Brandy's mind to see Zane turn on her. He dared to tell Sherita he needed to get away from Brandy before she ruined his life. Brandy had problems, but she wasn't that unstable. He would say anything to get back in good with Sherita, and that made him weak. Unable to stomach it any longer, Brandy exited the car.

She was relieved the neighbors weren't outside listening to Zane talk horribly about her. People might get the wrong impression of her—that she wasn't smart. She despised people questioning her intelligence. Her learning pace was slower compared to others, but she was not dumb.

"Can we go, Zane?" Brandy asked with attitude. If she weren't desperate for his help during this difficult time in her life, she would've paid Sherita to keep him.

"Go back to the car," said Zane. "This ain't got nothing to do with you."

This had everything to do with her. Zane drove her car to Sherita's house, knowing the two didn't get along. He disrespected Brandy by telling Sherita about her business. What was it about Sherita that caught his attention? She wasn't as pretty as Brandy. Zane needed to learn his worth. Time in the foster care system hadn't been kind to him. He groveled before Aunt Sheila yesterday, and now Sherita.

"Listen to your friend," said Sherita to Zane.

"She said you can't stay here." Brandy touched Zane's arm to show support, but he pushed it away. Undeterred, Brandy said, "I got us. We'll be good." It was a huge ask, but the idea she had could work.

"You got us?" He laughed in Brandy's face. "Because of you... Forget it. I'm done repeating myself." He turned to Sherita, who walked away to take the boys inside. As Sherita prepared to close the door, Zane called after her. "Sherita, come back. We can work on us. I'm ready to be everything you need me to be. You don't have to worry about me on my game. Someone stole it. I'll get out of the streets for good this time." Taking his wallet from his pocket, he pulled out some money. "Let's take the boys shopping and get something to eat as a family."

Zane should've been ashamed of himself for saying he'd get out of the streets. They had a lot of money saved for the down payment of a house, but they had a way to go. As set on buying a home as Zane was, he wouldn't stop robbing. If Brandy had a bat, she would've hit him over the head for being weak. Yet, a part of her wished a man would beg for her love and affection. What happened next shocked her. Sherita took the money from Zane's hands and said she'd call him to talk about their family another day.

"What do you mean we'll talk later? I need a place to stay. You'd take my money and leave me homeless? That's what you think of me?"

Before closing the door in Zane's face, Sherita rattled off a list of things the kids needed. That was a cold-blooded demonstration, considering

Zane took care of his kids and had already given Sherita money this month. Brandy told Zane to stop, but to no avail. His kids were inside and probably scared. The boys had already seen him begging, and now this. If Zane kept it up, his kids wouldn't respect him.

And yet... this was the perfect opportunity to get back at him for mentioning Braelynn earlier. However, Brandy couldn't be so cruel, no matter how badly Zane had treated her for the past two days. She wanted to say his kids would be better off without him since he disrespected their mother and tried to break into their home. Although his name was still on the lease, Sherita didn't want him there. Zane loved her too much to get the landlord involved.

On the other side of the door, Sherita hollered at Zane, calling him names. The two were dysfunctional. This further infuriated Zane, who screamed every sexual thing Sherita had ever done to him as if he hadn't done equal or more disgusting things to her. Brandy stood back until he stopped beating at the door, which didn't take long because Sherita threatened to call the cops.

Furious at that threat, Zane continued, "The kids probably ain't even mine no way. If I can't see them, that means you got another nigga paying bills and taking care of your kids. You ain't got to worry about seeing me. Lose my number. Have your new man pick up where the fuck I left off. I want paternity tests, bitch, before I see them kids or give you another dime."

While walking to the car, Brandy contemplated what he had said. Zane's name should've been "Mr. Go Too Far." What he said was disgusting, even if he didn't mean it. She'd never be friends with a man who didn't take care of his kids. Knowing Zane, he'd process things later and blow up Sherita's phone, apologizing. Brandy hadn't thought of it until now, but Zane needed to be in anger management.

Inside the car, she said, "You may not want to hear it, but I got a major scheme. We can live rent-free. No hotel-hopping and no sleeping in the car."

"Stop acting like I'm a goofy. Drop me at a hotel, and then you can keep going."

It would take more convincing to persuade him. Ignoring Zane's frustrated expressions, Brandy turned off the music and begged him to hear her out.

Finally, he relented. "Speak, and it better be good."

As he listened, Zane expressed concerns, prompting them to brainstorm ways to address potential issues. Other than that, he was completely on board. Rather than drive to a hotel, they went to the gas station and got snacks and drinks. Brandy needed something to swallow her medication. If they were going to pull off the mission, she had to be medicated. Thankfully, her pills had been in her purse and not the stolen bags. Next stop: Walmart to get rope and tape.

5

BRANDY

AFTER LEAVING WALMART, THEY parked on a dead-end street in Gary, far away from the only house on the block. Near the house was a wooded area, perfect for burying bodies. The only other building on the street was an abandoned call center. Tall grass covered the land where houses once stood. Brandy hadn't known this street existed until she began delivering food. It was the perfect location to pull off Brandy's scheme.

The client, whom Brandy knew by the initials of C.B., could use a lawn care service. The grass was long and full of weeds. The two-story house looked like it had seen better days. It could've used a fresh coat of paint. Maybe the inside of the house looked better; Brandy hated a dirty home. Since C.B. had agoraphobia, taking care of her mental health likely trumped caring for her property. Brandy stopped being so judgmental because she understood mental illness.

For hours, they waited at the end of the block to verify if Brandy was right about C.B. not having visitors except delivery people. No one had come into or out of C.B.'s house, and there were no deliveries. The only activity was the few cars passing by on the primary avenue. Nothing would stop them from successfully pulling off their plan. It was now dark enough for them to approach the house.

While putting on his face mask, Zane said, "This is a good plan, but staying at a motel for a few more nights will give us more time to watch the house. We're moving too fast."

Brandy disagreed, "Trust me, no one loves her. She has no visitors. We're here, so we might as well do it now."

Zane looked uncertain. He said, "I don't know. Can I count on you to stay on your medication so we can keep our eyes on that female? The last thing we need is for her to get out of your sight when I'm at work and stab or shoot you with a weapon we didn't know she had."

"I took my medication in front of you earlier. But to answer your question, I'll take it consistently."

When Zane nodded, she put on her mask and shoved the rope and tape in a backpack she bought from Walmart. They drove to the alley behind C.B.'s house, broke the lock on the empty garage, and parked the car inside. After exiting the garage, they approached the house and searched for an effortless way to get in. Since there were bars on the windows, Zane kicked in the flimsy back door. C.B. didn't care much about safety. No alarms made it easy to break into the garage and house.

Please don't let C.B. have animals or guns. We outnumber her, but we can never be too safe, Brandy thought.

With guns drawn, they crept through the dark kitchen, ready for anything. A dim night light barely lit the dining room, but Zane still crashed into a table. Brandy heard something scurrying, even though C.B.—and any animals—were nowhere around. If C.B. kept vicious dogs, they'd have to go. Brandy had never understood the appeal. Dogs bit people, and she wasn't about to get mauled. Cats, though—they could stay.

Zane turned on the light when they entered the living room. Brandy was taken aback by the house's surprising interior. Despite not expecting much, what she saw was unbelievable. The cushions on the wooden furniture appeared to be of good quality, but they were from a bygone era. The walls and end tables displayed images of a slim, attractive, white woman with blond hair and blue eyes, dressed in Western clothing. Brandy believed that the woman in the picture was C.B., as she had only glimpsed C.B.'s arm while she collected her food. C.B. must have had a lot of self-confidence to have many pictures of herself on display. Vain women were just as despised by Brandy as flies. C.B.'s residence would have fit perfectly in a museum dedicated to the Civil War. The fall and Halloween decorations clashed with the Civil War theme in the living room. Someone needed to teach C.B. how to decorate.

Pointing at the stairs, Zane motioned for Brandy to follow him. She prepared herself. C.B. could've heard them break in and waited upstairs with a firearm, ready to blast them away. Or she could've called the police. Neither of them had been to jail or prison, and Brandy desired to keep it that way.

Brandy counted four doors once upstairs in the dark hallway. She had to stay vigilant, eyes scanning everything around her. C.B. or a pitbull could barrel out of any door. Zane headed to the first closed door where a TV played. The only light came from the TV. Brandy kept hearing what sounded like small animals running about. In a hushed tone, Zane asked Brandy if she had noticed the sound.

She whispered back, "It wouldn't surprise me if this weird chick had a house full of cats."

"We'll know soon what the hell that noise is. Ready?" When she nodded, Zane opened the door.

Both entered with their guns raised. C.B. sat in her bed watching TV with a nightgown on. When she noticed them, fear took over, and she reached for the phone on her nightstand.

"I wouldn't do that if I were you." Zane sounded like a tough guy in a gangster film.

"We've killed before and ain't afraid to do it again," Brandy lied to show dominance.

C.B. slowly raised her hands in surrender. "I don't know what y'all want. But you can see from downstairs and upstairs, I don't have many valuables. Take whatever you want. I don't have cash. I promise I'll sit here and won't move." Brandy couldn't place the state where C.B. was from, but she had a Southern accent.

Brandy chuckled. Poor C.B. didn't know why they were there. Why would she suspect people had broken into her house and taken her hostage? When Zane sat on the bed, C.B. moved away from him.

He leaned toward C.B., placing his hand on her knee, and said, "I'm not here for pussy. My friend and I need a place to stay for a little while, and you'll be hosting us. If you understand, nod."

"Take whatever you want." C.B. looked confused. "There must be better places you can stay. This house needs so many repairs, and—"

Brandy cut her off, "What's your name?"

C.B. said, "Carlotta Buchanan. Pawning my TVs and costume jewelry should give you enough money for a hotel."

"Shut up," said Brandy, who joined Zane and Carlotta on the king-size bed. "You must think we're stupid. We don't need you to think of a plan for us. We did that before coming here, and your house was the best choice."

That quieted Carlotta.

"Listen to my friend," Zane said. "You are our best and only option. Go along with the plan, and you'll make it out of this alive. We're not here to steal, because we ain't thieves."

Why had Zane lied? If Brandy found anything worth pawning, she'd steal it. However, nothing looked valuable. Granted, they hadn't searched the entire house. Brandy and Zane removed their masks and gloves. While still in the car, they had agreed to murder Carlotta before permanently departing from her home. They were uncertain about the duration of their stay. Once they created a monthly budget, they'd know. Though Brandy consented to killing Carlotta, she hadn't been serious and didn't believe Zane was either. But he had reasoned killing Carlotta would prevent them from getting caught.

Carlotta asked reasonable questions that they refused to answer. How did they find her? Why her house? How long would they stay? She talked too much for Brandy's liking. After the first few unanswered questions, one would think she'd shut her mouth.

Brandy questioned Carlotta about the possibility of having visitors in the future, excluding delivery people. When Carlotta shook her head, she ordered Carlotta to hand over all her weapons and cell phones. Zane removed the telephone cord from the wall and placed it in his pocket. He didn't wait for Carlotta to show him around her room. He opened her drawers and went through her things, searching for phones, computers, and weapons. Carlotta's walk-in closet looked like a movie dressing room for a woman playing the role of a plantation wife. The hats, umbrellas, colorful puffy dresses, and shoes should've been in the Civil War Museum. Very few clothes folded on the shelf belonged to this generation: jogger pants, shorts, and t-shirts. Even the lace on Carlotta's sheer nightgown looked dated. Brandy would have to figure out why Carlotta was weird later.

When they found no electronics or weapons, they walked Carlotta to each room in the house. Brandy held the gun against Carlotta's back as Zane searched through her things. Carlotta revealed two bats kept in the closet of one of the guest rooms, and Zane took them. Despite her efforts,

Brandy had yet to come across anything worth stealing. Men's clothes overflowed the closets and drawers in both spare rooms.

"Who do these clothes belong to?" asked Zane. "Should we be expecting your man or brothers for a visit?"

"After buying this house, my parents and brother died in a car accident four years ago. I haven't been able to get rid of their things."

Brandy guessed she was telling the truth, but where were her mother's clothes? Perhaps Carlotta's mother was into old-time clothes, and when she died, Carlotta began wearing them. Brandy brushed it off because her mind went back to the noise they had heard earlier.

"How many animals do you have and what kinds?" Brandy asked Carlotta.

Confused, Carlotta said, "None."

Zane and Brandy stared at one another.

Zane said, "Then what was all that noise we heard downstairs and upstairs? Lie to me, and I'll kill your animals as soon as I spot 'em."

"I have rats, okay? It's nothing I'm proud to admit." Carlotta exhaled as if it took everything within her to admit this truth. "That's why it would be best if you all lived somewhere else."

Brandy was surprised that Carlotta, who was so attractive, had rats when there were many ways to exterminate them. Carlotta's mental illness appeared to be more serious than Brandy's. Perhaps Carlotta was correct. It would be best if she and Zane left. Brandy had no experience with living alongside roaches, mice, or rats, and had no intention of starting now.

She whispered to Zane, "I don't want to stay here with no damn rats. We'll stay at a hotel and figure things out."

"That's not happening. She's not scaring us away. We can solve the rat problem easily."

Brandy wasn't satisfied with his answer because she required a specific date and time for the problem to be resolved. It would be hard to sleep since they had to watch over Carlotta and worry about rats biting them.

Carlotta said to Zane, "Listen to your friend. This home is old. If getting rid of the rats was easy, honey, I would've done it long ago."

Tired of Carlotta's mouth, Brandy led Carlotta downstairs while poking her in the back with her gun. Zane followed and ordered Carlotta to hand over her electronics and all the sharp objects. Brandy gathered all potential weapons and brought them to the car, leaving nothing for Carlotta. If Brandy's parents were still alive, how would they react to her decision to take Carlotta as a hostage? Her father, if medicated, would've shaken his head and tried to talk sense into her. Her mother might've said it was risky, but she doubted her mother would've cared that Brandy planned to use someone. Her mother had made a living by setting up drug dealers. The woman never worked a traditional job.

Back in the house, they climbed into Carlotta's bed and forced her into the middle. It was odd for Brandy to sleep next to this stranger, and odder for Carlotta, who appeared stiff. To show compassion, Brandy reassured Carlotta that neither she nor Zane were sex perverts, so she might as well get some sleep. It took a while for Carlotta to close her eyes, and when she did, Zane told Brandy to watch Carlotta for two hours so he could sleep. This would prove easy. They had nothing to worry about. Carlotta had no access to the outside world and nothing to kill or injure them with. Brandy turned the TV from whatever Western show played and watched reality TV while she struggled to keep her eyes open. Not long after, she drifted off to sleep.

6

BRANDY

Zane's screaming woke Brandy.

Jerking upright in bed as Zane yelled, Brandy realized they were alone in the room. Where the hell was Carlotta? Zane reminded Brandy that she had failed again.

"Oh, no!" Brandy scrambled out of bed.

She had her gun on her; all she needed were her shoes. Thankfully, Carlotta hadn't taken Zane's gun either. He waved his gun in the air, threatening to shoot Brandy if the police came to the house. Zane continued to cuss as Brandy followed him down the hall to search for Carlotta. They searched the rooms and the bathroom. No Carlotta. When the fattest and longest rat Brandy had ever seen ran from underneath the bathtub, they hollered. Horrified that the rat would bite her, Brandy grabbed Zane, and he shoved her.

"You had one job and failed. I can't count on you to do nothing." Zane left the bathroom, and cautiously entered the hallway.

Pride made Brandy want to protest Zane's words, but she *had* failed him again. No wonder he didn't trust her. If they got killed or put in prison because of her, she'd never forgive herself. Why was she such a screw-up?

They crept downstairs, not knowing what to expect. Carlotta could be at the door with the police. Or fear could've healed her of agoraphobia, and she could've been long gone. Any way Brandy looked at it, she and Zane were fucked. Brandy noticed Carlotta crying on the floor near the front door as they approached the bottom of the stairs. There must have been a horrific reason Carlotta stayed in the house with her hostage-takers instead of going outside.

Zane ran to Carlotta pretending to be a gentleman. Carlotta wasn't going anywhere, so Brandy took her time getting to her. Zane should've congratulated Brandy for a job well done instead of attending to Carlotta. Although Brandy had made careless mistakes, she got one thing right: she picked the right person to take advantage of.

While Zane lifted Carlotta from the ground, Brandy closed the living room windows and kept her eyes open for rats. The windows were closed last night. Carlotta must have opened them this morning to get the attention of a delivery person. Carlotta thought she was smart, but Brandy would outsmart her.

When Brandy saw Carlotta's dress, she laughed and pointed at the hideous thing. It was a pink and white striped, long-sleeved, multi-tiered dress with black lace around each tier. Peeing must've been a chore. To Brandy's surprise, no Confederate flags waved in the house.

Brandy needed answers about the dress, but it would have to wait. Carlotta had to be put in her place, and Brandy was the person to do it. "If you try what you did again, I'll shoot you. We're not playing games. Keep the windows closed. Do you understand?"

Carlotta wiped her tears and nodded while Zane dusted off her dress. Carlotta's home was rat-infested; she wasn't dainty. A girly girl would've never lived with rodents. Brandy didn't like the attention Zane gave Carlotta. He hadn't attempted to dust Brandy off when he slammed her to the ground at the motel. He needed to focus and not treat Carlotta delicately because she was pretty. The woman was mental, and Brandy hoped Zane realized it. They would need to talk privately if he got any softer.

After Brandy motioned for Carlotta to sit, Carlotta sat in her rocking chair staring at them, who sat on the couch opposite her.

Carlotta said, "You all won't have any more problems out of me. I have no choice but to accept we're roommates until you all say otherwise, so I'll make the most of it."

Zane smiled hard at Carlotta and said, "We're not here to hurt you. Just go about your life, and we won't be a problem."

A gigantic rat ran from the dining room into the living room. Zane and Brandy screamed and jumped onto the couch. This time, it was Carlotta who laughed and pointed. Brandy disliked Carlotta making fun of them as if they were idiots. Carlotta removed her ankle boot, adorned with ribbons and tassels, and hurled it at the rat. Into the fireplace, the rodent went.

Marching to the fireplace, Carlotta proved herself to be a rat whisperer, "Get your tail out of there," she said to the rat. "Now!"

The rat must've understood English because it ran to the back of the house.

"How come your house is clean and you have rats?" Brandy asked Carlotta. "It ain't adding up."

"The house is old," said Carlotta, now back in her rocking chair. "It needs repairs to stop them jokers from getting inside. I'm open to suggestions if you have any. Y'all can stop standing on the sofa; the rat is gone. It's more scared of you than you are of it."

Embarrassed, they sat. This wasn't Brandy's first time in an older house that needed repairs. Carlotta needed a house that was not located close to the woods, possibly resolving the rat problem.

"Brandy, we need to talk." Zane stood and motioned for her to speak with him in the dining room, where he whispered, "I'm not working today.

Stay here while I buy some rat traps, locks for Carlotta's door, handcuffs, and clothes. I don't trust you to go shopping because you'll overspend. Don't fuck up while I'm gone." He pointed in the living room toward Carlotta. "She can live with rats, but not me."

Since Zane reminded her of how she'd been messing up, she put the focus on him. "You don't have to worry about me. I'm about to take my medicine. Make sure Carlotta doesn't make you soft. I saw how you were dusting her off."

Making Brandy uncomfortable, Zane got in her face. "Look at your history and look at mine." The smirk he gave her made her want to wipe it off his face. "I'll be back." He was out the door.

"I guess it's just us." Carlotta joined her in the dining room. "I don't know about you, but I'm hungry. Since you're my babysitter, come watch me cook." She headed to the kitchen with Brandy in tow.

At the table in the kitchen, Brandy sat in the chair with her legs underneath her so a rat wouldn't run across her shoes. Carlotta pulled out a cast-iron pot and rinsed it at the sink before rolling up her sleeves and putting on an apron. Brandy assumed Carlotta would want to change clothes to get comfortable, but she was wrong.

"What do you do for a living?" asked Carlotta, who placed a bowl of water and green beans on the table before sitting next to Brandy.

How could Carlotta cook in this house? Brandy would never store food here or use the kitchen to cook. Instead of answering Carlotta, Brandy stared at her.

"You're not big on conversations. That makes sense seeing how we met. You're welcome to eat with me."

"You're nasty as hell for eating in this place. Aren't you scared of rats dropping turds into your food?"

"The rats and I have an understanding." Carlotta grinned. "They don't touch my food." She opened a small closet that Brandy and Zane missed last night when they checked for weapons and electronics. Carlotta pulled out the broom and twirled it. "I hit them with this, and they run." The crazy woman swung the broom like it was a samurai sword.

In case Carlotta got the idea to hit Brandy with the broom, she patted her gun tucked inside her skirt.

"Calm down. I was having a little fun. I have to keep myself entertained in this house." After putting away the broom, Carlotta snapped green beans.

"Why do you dress like that? You must be in your thirties," Brandy said, eying Carlotta's clothes and boots.

"A lady never tells her age." Carlotta looked at her dress as if she were proud. "The Civil War era was a more peaceful time. I love everything about that period except for slavery. Black people deserve reparations. I don't know why your people don't push harder for it."

Carlotta must've assumed she was stupid. "Don't lie. You hate niggas." Carlotta's family probably owned slaves. This was the first time Brandy had heard a White person say Black people deserved reparations.

"If I didn't like Blacks, why would I move to Gary?"

That was Brandy's question. How had the woman come to Gary, a predominantly Black city?

When Brandy asked what brought Carlotta to the city, she said, "My family wanted a change from living in the south. I'm from a small town in Tennessee. When my father's friend put this house up for sale, my parents bought it since it's near Chicago and Lake Michigan." Her father probably stole the house from a Black person, but Brandy kept that to herself. Carlotta wouldn't admit it if it were true.

Brandy kept her promise to Zane by sipping water from the sink minutes later to take her medicine. Carlotta looked offended when Brandy refused to drink from a glass. While Carlotta cooked, Brandy messaged Zane about purchasing bins for storage purposes. The rats would destroy anything that was left out. Despite the absence of holes in Carlotta's dress and boots, Brandy wasn't willing to jeopardize her possessions.

Carlotta put her greens on the stove and then soaked the pinto beans. Facing Brandy, she said, "Would you like me to hem and take out a few of my dresses for you? I assume you saw my sewing machine. It wouldn't be any trouble." Carlotta was approximately five feet nine inches and one hundred thirty-five pounds. She and Brandy were completely different in terms of their physical build.

"I'll pass," said Brandy, wondering what vibe she'd given off that would make Carlotta assume Brandy would wear her clothes.

When Carlotta sat next to Brandy, Carlotta asked, "Do you have hobbies?" Brandy picked underneath her nails, ignoring the question. Carlotta sighed. "You don't have to be cold. I never get visitors and I thought we could talk. Telling me your hobbies won't help me identify you if the police show up."

Maybe Carlotta had a point. It couldn't help sharing harmless things. "I like to do my makeup, but someone stole it. Nothing special." Why did she say nothing special? Carlotta might believe she lacked self-confidence. "I got other talents, but enough about me," she lied. Brandy hadn't figured out what she liked to do.

"I wish I had makeup here. I'd let you do mine. My hobby is writing fiction. I'm an author." Embarrassed, Carlotta covered her face. "I've never said I'm an author out loud."

Bored and hungry, Brandy pretended to care. "What kind of books do you write?"

"My first short story is almost done, and I think it's horror, but I'm not sure."

Carlotta must've lied about being an author. This was a trick to get her laptop back so she could alert the cops.

Turning on the oven, Carlotta said, "The rats ate through the bottom of the oven, and sometimes it takes a while to heat. I'll have to get a new one soon."

Brandy examined the stove, and it indeed had holes. All she could do was frown and shake her head.

Minutes later, Carlotta asked, "Will you be the first person to read my book?" She stared at Brandy, waiting for a response.

Brandy had never enjoyed reading. When teachers would call on her to read, she asked for a restroom pass. She could read, but not well. "I don't read. I know what you're trying to do. You think I'm going to give you your laptop, but I'm not, so you can stop pretending you wrote a book."

"I handwrote it. My notebook is upstairs." She placed her hands in a prayer position. "Let me read it to you. Give me your honest feedback. I can take it."

Brandy pulled out her phone to see the time. Zane needed to get back soon. Carlotta was working on her nerves.

"If it's trash, I'll break your ankles." Brandy laughed. "I saw *Misery* by Stephen King."

Carlotta chuckled. "It's not a masterpiece because it's my first book, so keep that in mind."

When Carlotta attempted to grab Brandy's arm to lead her upstairs, Brandy stepped back and upped her weapon. Carlotta got the message, and they headed upstairs where Carlotta got her notebook from the closet. Brandy wouldn't allow Carlotta to lead her around the house like they were friends. Not a stranger to loss, a part of Brandy had compassion for

Carlotta. She'd let the woman have some fun, but Brandy would shoot her if she tried anything.

Shortly after, Carlotta took a seat at the dining room table and eagerly opened her notebook. She mentioned the story had no title and inquired if Brandy was comfortable hearing about murder, child abuse, rape, and torture. Upon hearing Brandy's declaration of fearlessness, Carlotta eagerly rubbed her hands together.

7

CARLOTTA'S STORY

1991

ON A CHILLY DAY *in Pigeon Forge, Tennessee, a militia hosted their week-ly meeting in a one-story building built by the members. The group and their families lived off the grid because America was no longer a place that put Americans first. The foreigners had taken over. At every meeting, Tom Sawyer, a muscular man with blond hair styled in a military cut, stood in the back and watched the door. He wore his bulletproof vest and gun in case the United States government came after the group. Because of his desire to protect America, he possessed a radical mindset. The government might've labeled Tom a threat had they discovered his actions. But Tom wouldn't allow the military to do to the militia what they did to David Koresh.*

Tom stared at the front of the room as the leader opened the floor. He became irritated when the leader said, "I have bad news."

That could've only meant one thing. The operation the group had been working on for months would not happen, and the planning had been a waste of time. Tom was getting ahead of himself. He'd let the leader talk, but if things didn't sound like Tom desired, he wouldn't be quiet about it. Normally, he remained respectful, but he had grown tired of the group being more talk than action.

Tom prided himself on being a man of few words. He was a model member. He had a good-looking wife, Trixie, who adored his dirty drawls and raised his children the way he wanted them raised. Many modern women went against what their husbands wanted when raising kids, but not good old Trixie. Tom said no religion, and that was the law. He didn't want his son raised soft, and his wife obeyed. He said the girl should be treated more leniently than her brother, but not too softly. Trixie complied. Tom needed sex four nights per week, and Trixie made sure it happened. He was a lucky man.

The leader continued, "I'm sorry to say this, but now isn't the time to go on a killing spree. Something tells me if we do it so soon after leaving the bomb in the trash can downtown, people will suspect it's us. Although there was some talk in town that the Klan did it, my source says people are asking if it could've been us."

Many of the thirty people in the crowd groaned, but Tom suspected most were relieved. Had it not been for him and Trixie, the bomb downtown wouldn't have happened. Many talked big, but their bark was bigger than their bite. It was Tom and Trixie who planted the bomb that another member had made. The men should've been ashamed that Trixie was the one who had the balls to pull off the mission. Tom's comrades weren't as concerned as he and Trixie were about foreigners taking over American jobs. Downtown businesses were notorious these days for hiring foreigners.

The mission with Trixie was a success; they didn't get caught. One foreigner's arm had been blown off, yet he survived. Tom desired more casualties since the bomb went off during a weekday when most downtown workers went for lunch.

Tom was the muscle for the militia, but he should've been the brains. He'd had enough. "Fuck this!" he interrupted. "Are we men or mice? Rise, men. Who's with me?"

The leader looked stunned at Tom's boldness and said, "You're angry, but the timing is off. Do you trust me, brother?"

"I don't. Either we put fear in the rich and their families like we agreed, or I'm out. If we don't show wealthy folks who give our jobs to foreigners that there are consequences for their actions, nothing will change."

The crowd watched the back and forth but remained silent. Trixie put a fist in the air in solidarity, and Tom's children, Alex, Cord, and Tina, stared at one another, wide-eyed. Tom would talk to the kids later about not having a poker face. Alex was twelve years old, and Cord and Tina were ten. Cord was his nephew, his brother's son, but Tom loved him like a son. Tom's brother and his wife were once a part of the militia. Five years ago, when everyone was asleep, Tom's brother and sister-in-law packed their belongings and left Cord behind in their trailer with a note addressed to Tom. His brother claimed he and his wife were moving to Montana for a fresh start. They'd be back for Cord once they got settled. Those bastards. They never called, sent money, or visited.

"You're questioning my authority after being with me for nearly thirteen years," said the leader. "Maybe it's time you leave."

Tom was done with the militia anyway, but it hurt that his leader wanted him gone. He was valuable, and it pissed him off that his leader didn't see that. How could Tom have stayed with a group that wasn't big on action for so many years? All they had ever done was go from town to town and beat up privileged individuals who had fancy jewelry, cars, and clothes. The police never caught the militia because they were smart enough to do things away from home. Nothing they had done before compared to the violence of the bomb. Tom wanted more blood, but he would have to venture out alone to make it happen.

"Trixie, kids, let's get the hell out of here." His family met him at the door.

Some of his friends tried talking some sense into him. It was they who needed a reality check. His thinking had never been clearer. He didn't need his so-called brethren to help him fix America; he had Trixie and the kids for that.

When the leader broke off the meeting, Tom sent his family to their trailer to pack. He had unfinished business with the leader. He needed the names and addresses of the militia's potential victims. If the pussy members wouldn't put the list to use, he would. Entering the leader's office, Tom ignored him while he sat at his desk. Tom headed for the office cabinet to retrieve the documents.

"You can leave, but you're not taking anything with you," the leader said while Tom grabbed a folder and removed its contents. Now in front of Tom, the leader held out his hands for the documents. "Give me the paperwork. I'm asking kindly."

Tom hit his former leader so hard that the man fell and hit his head on the sofa. The glare he gave the man made him stay on the ground. A part of Tom was disgusted that he'd served a pussy who refused to fight back. Another part of him was proud that he stood up for what he believed in. As he exited the office, several men rushed inside, past Tom, and toward their leader. No one dared chase after Tom.

For several weeks, the Sawyer family slept at rest stops. The van was cramped, but they made it work. The trailer they once lived in belonged to the leader, so Tom left it there rather than have the leader involve the courts to get it back. He'd rather save money than stay in motels. Being uncomfortable wouldn't harm his family; he prepared them for war. It was a luxury to sleep in a bed at night, and until this point, they'd had it good. At least they had sleeping bags that fit in the back of the van. He was proud of his accomplishments. They still ate well, but much healthier meals than they had in the past. Trixie no longer cooked, which she enjoyed. The Sawyers ate fruit for breakfast and snacks, and meat and vegetables at night to ensure they stayed fit. What Tom prepared his family for, they couldn't be overweight. Their ability to escape on foot would soon become crucial for their survival.

The family had spent weeks planning an attack and were now prepared for their first victims. While they had never attempted something of this magnitude previously, their combined efforts made them unstoppable. Tom expected little input from the children because they were young, but their intelligence astonished him and Trixie. Now it was time to shock the King family.

8

CARLOTTA'S STORY

1991

ON HALLOWEEN NIGHT, THE family waited in their van at the end of a residential street while trick-or-treaters knocked at doors. The Sawyer family would wait until things died down; they didn't need witnesses. Halloween was a wicked night, no better holiday to do evil things. Tom and Trixie dressed as Gomez and Morticia Addams; Tina was Wednesday. Alex was Homer Simpson, and Cord dressed as Bart.

The home the family watched belonged to the one and only Rupert King and his family. Rupert was the owner of Famous Potato Chips and fired many Americans, only to hire foreigners for less pay. Rupert was a cheap son of a bitch with his workers, but he lived in a middle-class area, drove last year's Bentley, and his kids went to private school. Tom got a hard-on thinking about humbling the King family.

The family exited the vehicle once traffic was lighter on the street. Holding Halloween bags, they gathered on the sidewalk by the King family home, pretending to inspect their bags as Trixie knocked on Rupert's door. The Sawyers joined her on the steps when the front door was opened. Brandishing her weapon, Trixie forced Mrs. King to step back and permit the unwelcome guests to enter.

In the living room, Rupert and his wife held their hands up. Mrs. King cried and pleaded for her family's safety, especially her children, who were upstairs getting ready for bed. She promised to show Tom's family where the money was. Rupert was a coward who let his wife do all the talking.

Tired of Mrs. King, Tom said, "Do me a favor and shut up. Money isn't why we're here." He and Trixie laughed. "I'm lying. I'll take money, and much more."

Rupert grew some balls and stepped in front of his wife. "Take what you want and do whatever you want to me, but my family is off limits."

Trixie said, "You aren't in control. We are." She motioned for the Sawyer kids to have a seat on the leather sofa and said to them, "Grab the remote off the table and turn on the TV."

Seeing their children watch TV, Tom remembered Rupert's children and sent Trixie after them. Soon after, the King kids came downstairs blindfolded. Mrs. King and Rupert rushed toward their kids but stopped when Trixie and Tom pointed guns at them. Scared, the King children asked questions but relaxed when Trixie told them they were playing a Halloween game.

Tom ordered Alex and Cord to take the King kids to the sofa. Rupert's son was eight, and their daughter was six years of age. Earlier, Tom and Trixie assigned the Sawyer kids the job of monitoring the King children. It would be easy since the Sawyer kids were older. Although Tom and Trixie's children had never fought, they were taught how. There would come a day they'd have to get physical, but not today. Tom would preserve his children's innocence for a while longer. This period of their lives was for them to take notes and learn about the family business.

"Why are you all here?" screamed Rupert, as if he were talking to his work subordinates.

"Say something else, and I'll shoot you," said Trixie before addressing the children. "Turn the TV up."

"Let my children go," hollered Rupert above the TV. Frustrated, Trixie forced Rupert a few feet away into the hall that was in Tom's view. A single shot sounded. "Agh! You shot me!" Rupert hit the floor and held his right leg.

No longer terrified of the guns, Mrs. King ran to the hallway to join her husband. Though hysterical, she took off her t-shirt and made a tourniquet. Her skills surprised Tom because she was a stay-at-home mother with auburn hair, brown eyes, and pouty lips. Her breasts were too large for a woman with such a small frame. If Tom were a betting man, he'd guess Rupert paid for those tits. Mrs. King turned Tom on, and he didn't hide it from Trixie. He couldn't stop licking his lips at the woman. Trixie wasn't insecure. She knew she looked good: blond hair, blue eyes, and thin.

Tina asked, "Daddy, what was that noise?"

All the kids faced Tom.

"Someone popping firecrackers. Watch TV," said Tom. The kids followed the instructions, which caught Tom off guard as they believed his lie.

Since the game would start soon, Trixie took Mrs. King upstairs to get another shirt. The kids didn't need to see her breasts. Tom moved a sofa close to the hall entrance to shield Rupert from the children. Although Rupert wore a tourniquet, he whined like a baby.

Tom made everyone form a circle on the living room floor when Trixie and Mrs. King returned. The children came up with this game, and Tom appreciated them for it. The King family wouldn't see this coming. Being a good sport, Trixie went over to Rupert and said something to shut him up. No one enjoyed playing games while someone cried. Where was the fun in that?

"Let the games begin," said Tom. "King family. My family will ask you questions, and if you get them wrong, there will be consequences. Answering for others is cheating."

"This makes no sense. Why are you doing this?" Mrs. King sat her kids on her lap, holding onto them like the Sawyers would devour them.

The Sawyer kids had memorized their questions and the answers. They weren't in regular school, never had been. Tom and Trixie home-schooled them to keep them away from the poisonous behavior of typical American children. Tom smiled when Alex stood to ask the first question. It made Tom proud to see his son taking part in the family business.

Alex was the spitting image of his father: muscular, blond, blue-eyed, with a cleft chin. "The first question is for the father, but I can't see him." Alex approached the couch near the hall, but Tom stopped him. "I'll read it aloud, but it would've been better if I could see him. 'In what year did Christopher Columbus discover America?" shouted Alex—loud enough that if someone had been upstairs, they would've heard him.

"You must be kidding," Rupert said above a whisper, "1492. Now, can you all leave, please?"

"Want to get shot in the second or third leg?" Trixie asked, forgetting the children were nearby. She addressed the kids, "I'm joking. Pay me no mind."

Tom shook his head at Trixie. She had to be more careful. Keeping things moving, Tom called upon Cord, "You're up."

Knowing Cord, Tom might have to force him to read his question. The boy acted shy, but since Tom's blood ran through his veins, he knew he was no coward. One day, Cord would grow out of his shyness. Cord was a handsome, thin boy with brown hair and eyes. Trixie often teased Cord, telling him he belonged in modeling classes because, at a young age, he favored James Dean. Since then, Cord had worn his hair like the actor used to wear his. However, Tom wouldn't let anyone in his family do something as frivolous as modeling or acting.

Shocking Tom, Cord pointed at Rupert's son as if the boy could see him and asked, "What was the last state to join the United States? Huh! Your eyes are covered. I'm talking to you, Paulie."

Well damn, Cord had made a friend. Not even Tom had remembered the boy's name.

"I don't know. I don't know!" shouted Paulie, who remained blindfolded. The boy sounded fearful. He must've picked up on what played out in the room. Tom loved children and hated to see them unhappy.

"Hawaii," Mrs. King blurted out and then hugged her kids.

"You cheated, Mrs. King, but I'll let it slide since that's your baby." To make the game livelier, Tom cheered and motivated his family to do the same for Mrs. King, who was a protective mother.

"You're getting soft on me," said Trixie, blowing Tom a kiss.

After catching his wife's kiss, Tom said, "It's my turn to ask a question." Tom pointed at Mrs. King. Desperate to punish the King family, he wanted Mrs. King to get the answer wrong. "What's the least populous state in the U.S.?"

All eyes were on Mrs. King, who appeared lost. When she called out to Rupert for help, Trixie warned her to stop cheating. Tom had forgotten Rupert was behind the couch. He peeked back there, and Rupert was falling asleep. They had to move the game along.

To prevent Rupert from falling asleep, Tom directed his wife to apply wet towels and ice cubes to his face.

When Trixie left the room, Tina caught Tom's enthusiasm. Tina said to Tom, "I know the answer, Daddy." Tina shook her brother, Cord, and taunted him. "I bet you don't know it."

"Hush, Tina," said Tom to his baby girl. "You created the question, so we know you know, but does Mrs. King?"

"You're a meany, Daddy." Tina pulled a hair tie from her pants pocket and slipped her blond hair into a ponytail.

"Do you have an answer, Mrs. King?" asked Tom.

"Maine, no, no, I meant—" said Mrs. King.

"She's cheating, Daddy." Tina wagged her finger at Mrs. King. "One answer per person."

"You're right, baby. She's cheating." Trixie entered the room, wiping her wet hands on her clothes. She addressed Tom, "Rupert's fine."

"The answer is Wyoming." Tom removed the King children from their mother's lap, placed them on the couch, and instructed his children to watch them. The King kids cried but calmed down when Tina promised to play a game with them.

As Tom offered his hand to Mrs. King, who was still on the floor, she avoided his gaze; he helped her up and guided her to the dining room for some privacy. A wooden door to the dining area kept the children from seeing what happened next.

Inside the room, Mrs. King resisted following Tom's instructions until he pulled out his gun and threatened to kill her family. He'd only asked her to do things he assumed her husband often asked of her. When Tom left Mrs. King in the dining room to head to the living room, he was certain her breasts were fake.

The Sawyer kids and Trixie asked the King children history questions in the living room. Rupert should've gotten a refund for the money he spent on private schools because his children were dumb as rocks.

Next, Trixie went to the dining room to spend time with Mrs. King while Tom stayed with the kids. After Mrs. King screamed loud enough for everyone to hear her, Tom reassured the children that she and Trixie were scaring one another. All the kids asked if they could go to the dining room, but Tom told them an adult game was being played in there. He gave the children the candy he found in the kitchen, and that kept them quiet.

Tom wondered what Trixie had done to make Mrs. King holler like that. Trixie had a dark side that not even Tom enjoyed encountering. She once fought Cord's biological mother and whooped her black and blue. Not your *typical girl hair-pulling match. Trixie had boxed like she expected to win cash at the end of the night.*

He left the kids on the couch and joined Rupert. To prevent Rupert from sleeping, Tom smacked him. "What year did Texas become a state? You fat, chip-eating prick."

"Ahh! I don't know. Stop torturing my family, fucking tell me what you want," Rupert screamed. "Leave! Now!"

When the Sawyer children asked what was wrong, Tom reassured them that Rupert's yelling was part of the game. They had nothing to worry about. He wasn't sure if his children bought that or not, but they stopped asking questions. He could hear the King kids crying, while his children soothed them.

Tom wagged his gun at Rupert and said, "You still don't get it. Rich people like you never do. Sorry to tell you, but there's more to life than money."

Rupert screamed and called out for his children to run. The King kids' cries grew louder; they couldn't be soothed. Next time, Tom would have his children take the victims' kids far away from the action. Undeterred, Tom dragged Rupert's body to the kitchen at the back of the house. Although Rupert resisted by grabbing rugs and doors, he was no match for Tom. Alex called out, asking if everything was fine. He must've heard Rupert resisting and fighting for his life. Tom told Alex to stick to the plan and watch the King kids; he and Rupert were creating a scary film.

Tom closed the kitchen door and turned up the volume of the radio on the counter. Two people had entered the kitchen alive. Only one exited alive. Tom reassured himself that he wasn't gay. Rupert deserved a lesson. Tom was in charge. Tom had engaged in sexual activity with men before. He used to have sex with his male cousins when he was younger.

Back in the living room, Trixie whispered into Tom's ear, "It's done."

Tom knew what that meant. Only one person survived the dining room rumble. He kissed Trixie on the cheek and told her to put the King children to bed. Once she did what Tom asked of her, she and Tom filled their Halloween sacks with money, candy, jewelry, and food.

"Let's rock-n-roll," said Tom, ready to go.

"Can we say goodbye to the mama and daddy?" Tina asked Trixie.

"They're sleeping," lied Trixie.

Upon exiting the King house, the family stepped out into the dark, quiet street. Tom drove the entire night. Sleeping at the rest stop was too risky; someone might've seen them leaving the King house. When the family debriefed, the kids said they got bored from sitting with the Sawyer kids who were younger, and next time they wanted to make people scream. They believed the lies about recreating a Halloween movie and playing an adult scary game. The children eagerly anticipated creating new Halloween trivia. Trixie then explained how studying history would help them ask better questions next year.

9

BRANDY

CARLOTTA'S STORY CAUGHT BRANDY off guard. The woman was mental. There was no other explanation for her writing such a story. As soon as Tom and Trixie brought up the topic of kids in the house, Brandy had a gut feeling that Tom would kill the children. Because Brandy was a parent, she felt sad for the King children. Unlike Rupert and Mrs. King, Brandy was alive but did a lousy job of parenting. She resolved that she would stop at nothing to be with Braelynn; not even bipolar disorder would get in the way. Her time on Earth was limited, and she could be taken from her daughter at any moment. If Brandy were to die at this moment, she would leave Braelynn with only memories of being abandoned. Brandy couldn't allow that to happen. If her parents watched over her from heaven, they'd be disappointed. She'd strive to make them proud from now on.

"People like the stuff you write?" She eyed Carlotta. Although the story had disturbing aspects, Carlotta's talent made Brandy remember just how talentless she was.

No matter how much Brandy wanted to act nonchalant, she couldn't lie; she liked the story and had questions. How did Tom and his wife get so vicious? Would the family get caught? How would the children turn out? To have their kids in the home while they tortured Rupert and Mrs. King was insane. She yearned to know what happened next.

"I saw your reactions when I read it. You liked it. Admit it." Carlotta beamed with pride.

"Some parts held my attention more than others. I'll give that to you." The story had been engaging, but Carlotta didn't have to know.

"Can I read more another day?" As Carlotta closed her notebook, she looked at Brandy with expectation, not understanding that Brandy had downplayed her talent.

"When I have nothing better to do, sure," Brandy sighed.

Seconds later, she followed Carlotta into the kitchen and gasped. She had to get out of this house. Carlotta yelled at the largest rat Brandy had ever seen walking across the counter near the stove. Luckily, lids covered the pots on the stove.

Screaming, Brandy ran from the kitchen into the living room, as far away from the rat as possible. While she surveyed the room for more rats, Zane texted saying to meet him at the car. After helping him carry the bags inside, Brandy stayed with Carlotta until she finished cooking. Zane left them downstairs while he installed a lock on Carlotta's door that locked from the outside. Once finished, he joined them in the kitchen.

To Brandy's surprise, Carlotta asked the unthinkable, "Would you all have a meal with me? If you tell me your favorite foods, I'll cook them."

"I haven't eaten all day. Can I help with anything?" Zane licked his lips.

Had Brandy heard him correctly? Despite not being informed about the rat, he had witnessed them inside the house and should have avoided eating Carlotta's food. Zane needed to keep his head on a swivel rather than become friendly with Carlotta.

Over dinner, Zane and Carlotta chatted like old friends. Brandy watched a movie on her phone in the living room and listened to their conversation. Carlotta's dining room and living room was an open-concept floor plan. They talked about old Western movies and characters they enjoyed. Zane had told Brandy years ago that he bonded with the foster home house manager by watching old movies and TV shows. Carlotta laughed like everything Zane said was hilarious. He wasn't that funny. Brandy should know. Brandy couldn't wait to confront him later. He was quick to tell her when she screwed up, so it was only right she returned the favor.

With a mouthful of food, Zane said to Brandy, "You sure you don't want none of these green beans, cornbread, greens, oxtails, and beans? Whew. Hmm. It's bussin'."

"I assume that means you like my food, sweetie," said Carlotta to Zane, sounding more country than normal. "That makes me smile."

Zane should've choked on a rat turd. Rather than tell him that, Brandy declined his offer.

Not long after, Zane handcuffed and locked Carlotta in her room so he and Brandy could go to the bathroom. Despite Zane's efforts to place rat traps around the house, they still felt scared to use the restroom alone. Since Zane purchased her new clothes, she'd return to work tonight. Unfortunately, Carlotta was no longer her client; she'd been a good tipper. Brandy found it strange that Carlotta was unaware that her grocery deliverer was the one who took her hostage. But why would Carlotta know? Carlotta was too frightened to fully open her door and meet Brandy, so she had never seen her face. The only thing she did was stick her arm out the door to get her stuff.

While Brandy soaked in the tub, Zane sat on the toilet and stared at the black-and-white pictures of Carlotta. Brandy gave him the benefit of the doubt. He focused on the photos to respect Brandy's privacy, but it wasn't like they hadn't seen one another naked before. At her Aunt Sheila's house, Brandy would sometimes walk in on Zane in the restroom, and he'd done the same to her. She never covered herself, but he always did. There he sat, acting shy. Had it been Carlotta in the tub, he wouldn't have been able to keep his eyes off her. Brandy dismissed that thought.

Still refusing to face her, Zane asked with an attitude, "Have you reached out to your daughter today?"

"I'm calling the county tomorrow to ask what I need to do to get Braelynn back. I had everything written down and lost it." Why did she admit to losing important information? She sounded unfit. "I'll call her."

"She'll be happy to hear from you. Having no contact with your family is hard. She deserves better." Zane's frustration caused her to wonder if this was about Braelynn or him growing up in foster care and not knowing about his family. "You need to get it together."

Although he was right, part of her still wanted to argue—because in that moment, she felt like a roach, and Zane was the boot coming down. They'd not had these problems when she was consistent in her daughter's life. Zane was far from the father of the year. He deserved to be held accountable for his actions too. Zane scrolled on his phone, not expecting a comeback.

"What you did at Sherita's house yesterday was bogus. Your kids should never see you like that. You scared them." She was nervous about sharing her thoughts, but she cared about Zane and his boys.

"I've been thinking about that today. I fucked up, but I'mma make it right." Zane dialed Sherita. She didn't answer, so he left a voicemail apologizing, promising to be better, and asking when he could see the kids. Surprisingly, he didn't mention getting back with Sherita in his message. The fact that he owned up to anything was unexpected.

"You've been in the tub long enough. I need a bath." Zane shook a bath towel at Brandy while he looked in the opposite direction.

"Take a bath with me. There's more than enough room. That way we'll finish together, unless you are cool staying in here by yourself."

"Hmm, nah, that's weird. Hurry. Stay in here with me until I finish, like I did for you."

After Brandy refused to wait for Zane to finish in the restroom, he got undressed while a smiling Brandy made room for him in the tub. Her plan worked.

"Stop looking me up and down."

Why did he have to be so overdramatic? She hated that she was that obvious, but his body was a work of art. He didn't work out, but he had abs and was skinny. The discoloration of his body bothered him, but not her. If only her best friend were more confident. To put him at ease, she covered her eyes until he sat behind her in the tub. Though it was risky, she used Zane's wash towel to wash his legs and feet. When he asked what she was doing, she instructed him to relax, and he obeyed minutes later. He must've been tired, because she just knew he'd kick her out of the tub. For reasons she couldn't understand, she had gotten turned on and desired his touch. They'd never be together. That was ridiculous. Yet she was desperate for a deeper connection. Turning around on her knees, she faced Zane and washed his shoulders and chest, ignoring his initial protests.

Caught in the moment, Brandy stared into Zane's brown eyes and said, "You're a god. You're enough. You're handsome."

Zane sucked his teeth. "Man, get your old soft ass outta here. Stop playing." He gently pushed Brandy's hand off his shoulder. "You sound like that maid from The Help. 'You is smart. You is kind.'" He kissed his teeth again. "Man."

"Nigga, be serious." Undeterred, Brandy placed her hand back on his shoulder. "You look perfect. Vitiligo looks good on you."

When he kissed her forehead unexpectedly, no words were necessary. Comfortable, she leaned back against him, and she became aroused when his manhood touched her. Overtaken by the moment, she grabbed Zane's dick.

"We don't do this." Zane gripped Brandy's wrist, ruining the mood.

Placing her finger over his lips, she said, "Think of it as a massage. This won't change anything between us. Lay your head back and let me do what I do."

"I'm in love with Sherita."

Why did he have to kill the vibe?

"I don't want you like that. I'm horny and you're here. Just one friend helping the other relax."

Although she fought the feeling, what she felt for Zane now had to be love. She'd never been in love with anyone. She dismissed thoughts of what it would be like to be Zane's woman. Whenever she was in a hypomanic episode, her sex drive went into overload. She'd taken her medicine; perhaps it needed a few more days to kick in. Zane and her sounded absurd together. Their friendship was known to everyone.

Unable to control herself, impulsivity took over. Brandy removed Zane's hand from her wrist and stroked his dick. All she wanted was to feel connected to another human. This wasn't lust or blurring the friendship line, was it? When his head fell backward, she knew he wouldn't give her any problems. She stared into the water, admiring the various shades of his dick. Vitiligo had affected every area of his body.

When he exploded, he looked blissful. If she didn't have to work, she'd text a man who would fulfill her sexual needs since Zane hadn't offered to return the favor. It would've satisfied Brandy had Zane said she pleased him, but he hadn't. As she reminisced about the facial expressions and moans that had escaped him, that was all the validation she needed.

While they dried off, she confronted Zane about being overly nice to Carlotta. He was adamant about not falling for their hostage. He said it wouldn't hurt to be nice since they had taken over the woman's house and were living rent-free. To deflect, he switched the conversation and lit up while saying how starting barber school soon would put them one step closer to home ownership. Brandy still hadn't decided on what she wanted to do with her life, but she vowed to herself to decide this week.

When Zane turned the doorknob to exit the bathroom, the door wouldn't open, so he tried again. Again. And again, but to no avail. He then beat on the door like that would help.

"What the hell is going on? Did you lock Carlotta's door?" asked Brandy.

"You were there with me, idiot." He screamed for Carlotta to let them out.

Had Carlotta outsmarted them?

10

BRANDY

ZANE'S PHONE SHOWED THAT three and a half hours had passed. Despite their continued cussing and screaming for Carlotta to let them out, they remained locked in the bathroom. Several times, Zane attempted to tear down the door without success. The only likely option out of the bathroom was to break the window and jump out of it. But neither wanted to break a bone.

They couldn't figure out how Carlotta had outwitted them. How had she locked them in the bathroom? Only they had the key to Carlotta's bedroom door, and it sat on top of the bathroom shelf. If Carlotta searched their belongings, she would've found their cell phones and called the police. They were prison-bound. Would it have taken three hours for the police to get to the house? Maybe the officers waited for backup, since this was a hostage situation. Or was Carlotta playing games? Maybe she was torturing them by leaving them locked in the bathroom before calling the cops to teach them a lesson. In case the police kicked in the door, Brandy and Zane put their guns in the cabinet so the officers would have no reason to shoot. Going to jail wrapped in a towel would be humiliating. She doubted the police would allow her and Zane to get dressed before carrying them out of the house.

Zane pulled on the doorknob again. Surprisingly, it opened. But how? She hadn't heard it unlock. What was going on? Confused, they stared at one another before Zane motioned for her to follow him.

Exiting the bathroom, they crept to Carlotta's room, expecting the police to jump out and handcuff them. But that didn't happen. Zane turned Carlotta's doorknob and found it locked. Using his key, he opened the door, and Carlotta was on the bed watching a black-and-white TV show.

Before they uttered a word, Carlotta said, "I heard you two screaming and figured you got locked in the restroom, but unfortunately, y'all locked me in here, and I couldn't help. I need a new restroom door lock because you have to wiggle the knob a certain way to open the door."

Zane said to Brandy, "This is crazy. From now on, we're keeping the bathroom door open."

For some unidentifiable reason, Brandy didn't believe Carlotta, and it surprised her that Zane had. Brandy pointed a finger at Carlotta. "You got out of this room, and I'll prove it."

"How could I? You two have the key. I'm watching *The Good, The Bad, and the Ugly*. Want to join me?"

Zane's towel only covered his lower body, leaving his chest exposed. Brandy noticed Carlotta staring at Zane's body, and when Carlotta saw Brandy watching her, she diverted her eyes.

Carlotta had better tread lightly. There'd be no captive falling for their captor while Brandy was around. Neither answered Carlotta. Brandy wasn't in the mood for entertainment. After getting locked in the bathroom, she'd have to start work later than she wanted, meaning her pockets would take a hit. Zane stood at the door watching the movie while Brandy searched Carlotta's walk-in closet for a hidden door. Nothing came of her efforts. Had she not needed to get dressed for work, she would have torn Carlotta's room apart until she found the secret door. She'd leave it for now, but this wasn't over. Fooling Zane was easy, but Brandy wasn't falling for Carlotta's charm.

***

Brandy spent the following day sleeping alone until noon in a guest room. When she arrived home from work past one o'clock in the morning, she discovered Zane sleeping in Carlotta's bed beside her. He refused to wake up when Brandy tried to wake him. It frustrated her that he hadn't kept his promise to sleep with her in one of the guest rooms. She thought it weird to keep sleeping with Carlotta. The first night, they did it to frighten and monitor Carlotta, but now that they had installed a lock on the bedroom door and purchased handcuffs, they no longer had to share a bed with her. Zane might have been sexually attracted to Carlotta. That might explain why he refused to leave her. Brandy was worrying too much. There must have been a reason behind his actions. He probably fell asleep while watching TV.

Since Zane left for work before Brandy awoke, she had no choice but to shower alone. Sleeping in the room alone had rattled her because of the rats, and now she had to do something else by herself. Fortunately for her, she hadn't come across a rodent, but the day was young.

After taking her medication, she removed the handcuffs from Carlotta, who brushed past her, heading to the restroom. Brandy couldn't help but shake her head in disbelief. Carlotta wore a sky-blue Victorian dress with white lace around the collar, sleeves, and hem.

Carlotta looked over her shoulder. "I almost peed myself waiting for you to unlock the door. I need a bell to get your attention."

The woman had some nerve. Brandy wished she would allow a white lady to ring bells at her. Who the hell did Carlotta think she was? Rather than respond, Brandy waved her off. While waiting for Carlotta to finish in the bathroom, a sound coming from the second guest room startled Brandy. She knew the sound but wouldn't go to investigate. It was a rat trap catching its prey.

Once Carlotta exited the restroom, she and Brandy went downstairs to get the dustpan, broom, and gloves. Brandy sent Carlotta into the room alone. Seconds later, Carlotta exited, holding the dustpan with a rat the size of a kitten. Carlotta tried to be funny and held the dustpan close to Brandy, causing her to jump away.

"You're terrified of rats." Carlotta chuckled, shaking her head.

"You better stop playing with me." Had Carlotta not been handling a rat, Brandy would've hit her.

After they went outside to dump it in the trash, Carlotta washed her hands and cooked.

While pouring butter beans into a bowl of water, Carlotta said to Brandy, "The beans need to soak for several hours. I'll cook them tonight, and we can eat them tomorrow. Zane will be hungry when he gets here, so I'll make something for us to eat this evening."

Brandy curled her lip in disgust. "If I wasn't clear the last time, I'm not eating your food. You don't have to worry about Zane. He delivers food. When he's hungry, he can get himself something to eat."

"But he likes my cooking, and you would too if you tried it." Carlotta's scowl pissed Brandy off.

Carlotta wasn't as nice as she pretended to be. It had only been a few times, but she had noticed Carlotta's unpleasant facial expressions. Carlotta tried to hide her initial reactions, but she couldn't get anything past Brandy.

Not interested in arguing, Brandy changed the subject. "What happens next in your story?" If she had to spend time with the woman, she might as well be entertained.

"I thought you'd never ask."

After Brandy accompanied her to get the notebook, Carlotta read more of her twisted tale.

CARLOTTA'S STORY

1999

ON HALLOWEEN, TOM PARKED the family van down the street from their next victims' house, waiting for the perfect time to attack. It would be dark soon, and then they'd strike the house on the corner with the large windows. Their victims wouldn't see them coming. They had lived a carefree life, as evidenced by having every shade open in the living room and dining room. It was unbelievable that some people could be so trusting. But the privileged always assumed they were above the violence that plagued other Americans. Tom knew all too well the dangers that lurked in the shadows. He and his family were the dark spots.

The Sawyer family still caused havoc in Tennessee. Tom had assumed their run would end, but apparently, his family was lucky. Pride swelled in him when he considered how everything had been working out for them since leaving the militia. One reason the family had been so successful was because they weren't blood-hungry. Once per year, they selected a well-to-do family to torture and kill. That way, they were less likely to get caught. And they never stayed in one location for long.

The now-grown children had become essential to the family business. It hadn't taken long for them to realize that what their parents did every

Halloween was far from fun and games. When Trixie and Tom finally explained their reasons, the children understood. In the end, the truth had helped.

Alex was twenty, and Tina and Cord were eighteen; all had graduated from homeschool with honors. The family made their money from robbing fast-food restaurants, gas stations, and unlucky citizens on the street. They were careful never to rob any place or person in the towns they currently stayed in.

Although favor now shone upon Tom, as a kid growing up in a trailer park in Franklin, Tennessee, he had felt unlucky. He'd often wondered if he was cursed. His single mother named him after a fictional character. She frequently kept a new guy between her legs and didn't have the decency to go to a hotel. In the family trailer, his mother screwed men so loud that Tom and his brother couldn't sleep. At a young age, Tom realized his mother was a whore, but it was years later when he learned the extent of her whoredom. One day, he heard her on the phone bragging to a friend about fucking men in the restrooms of local bars. That explained why men smirked at Tom whenever he went outside of his home.

Although his mother was loose, she kept food on the table. Not hot meals, because she hated cooking, but Tom and his brother had all the Wonder bread, bologna, chips, and juice they could dream of. His mother had her pleasant moments. She was just hot in the drawls, and that was why he kept a close eye on Tina, who had blossomed into a woman that boys and men couldn't keep their eyes off.

It had been a year since the family killed their last victims: a couple and their adult son who made the lives of fellow Americans pure hell. The Cranes had owned a plastic factory that made plastic utensils, and their employees often sued them for sexual harassment and for not paying fair wages. The entire Crane family were sex perverts. Despite their workers' protests, the

Cranes always came out successful in court. Tom couldn't prove it, but the Cranes had judges on their payroll. What happened to the Cranes had been horrible. The case remained unsolved.

Finally, it was dark enough outside for the Sawyers to execute their plan against the Al-Amins, a family that owned several gas stations across Jackson, Tennessee. The father, Matthew, began well as a business owner before he turned into a scumbag. He had initially hired Americans and trained them on how to run his gas stations, but after a few years, he fired all his employees for bogus reasons and replaced them with people who looked like him. After some investigation, Tom's family discovered the new employees at the gas station were related to the Al-Amins. Tom wouldn't have minded if the Al-Amins had hired some of their family members, but to fire all their employees was treacherous. The Al-Amins had to pay.

Tom told his family, "Put on your gloves. Let's rock and roll."

Tina was the first to exit the van, dressed as Cher from Clueless. She wore a cross-body purse containing her gun. These days, Tina and Trixie took turns going to their victims' doors and getting access to the house. Once Tina was inside, the rest of the family got out of the van and entered behind her. Stepping into the living room, Tom smiled with pride at his daughter, who pointed a gun at Matthew while his family stared in surprise. Matthew was a widower who shared his spacious home with his two sons, who managed several of the family gas stations. Mahdi was twenty-one and Amer was twenty-seven.

Alex, dressed like the wrestler Road Warrior Animal, closed all the blinds. What the family was about to do to the Al-Amins required privacy. Cord, who was dressed like John Travolta in Grease, *rummaged through the house, seeking phone cords to cut. Trixie, dressed like a slutty witch, stood with her daughter and trained her gun on the Al-Amins while they begged for their lives. After Trixie threatened to shoot every one of them, they shut up.*

Dressed as a vampire, Tom rearranged the furniture. It was best to sit on the floor in the middle of the living room to play the game. He admired the space, which was decorated with Halloween décor. It surprised him that the Al-Amins had mannequins dressed in costumes and skeletons in the corners of the living room. It was something people did when they had children, and the Al-Amins had none. People with money were wasteful. Tina tied their victims' hands, then Tom placed them on the floor in a circle. The games could begin.

Tom said to the victims, "From the looks on your faces, you have questions. The only thing you need to know is that my family judged your family as vampires. America let you into this country, and you pretended to be one of us, hiring good Americans so they could support their families. Then you showed your true nature and fired 'em all, sucking the motivation out of many of 'em."

Sitting next to Matthew Al-Amin, Trixie shoved his head and said, "I hate nepotism."

"Dad is being punished for securing a better life for his family. This is nonsense." Amer wiggled, trying to get loose from the rope that tied his hands.

Matthew yelled, "Let my sons go! Every decision was mine alone. I'm the owner."

"Excuses, excuses." Trixie squeezed Matthew's cock through his dress slacks until he screamed. "I bet the people you fired screamed like that while in the unemployment line."

The Sawyer children clapped. They loved a good show. And Tom and Trixie knew how to entertain.

"I'm too young to die," said Mahdi, the younger son, crying like a bitch. "This is my senior year in college, and I haven't lived. My girlfriend will get suspicious if I don't meet her later. I won't say a thing. Do whatever you want

with my brother and father. My father killed my mother. And my brother is the asshole who helped him cover it up."

There had been suspicions that Matthew killed his wife while hiking on their wedding anniversary. Somehow, his wife fell off a cliff while Matthew snapped a picture of her. The detectives couldn't prove it was foul play, though they wondered why Matthew's wife took a picture so close to the edge. Matthew, who made good money, inherited a good sum of money after claiming his wife's life insurance. The bastard must've been cheap because he lived in a middle-class neighborhood rather than a mini mansion like Tom had suspected.

"Fucking traitor! All I do for you, and this is how you reward the family?" Matthew glared at Mahdi as if he'd beat him if he could.

When Amer opened his mouth to say something, Alex rained punches on him. Amer moaned and begged for his life, only for Alex to kick him. It was as if Alex had read Tom's mind. Tom hadn't time for the family feud, it was time to play the game.

"If you kill my son, I'll kill you," Matthew threatened Alex, as if he were a flunky who worked for him.

Alex smirked and ignored Matthew. Mahdi kept quiet, assuming silence would save his life.

"You're powerless," said Tom to Matthew. Tom pointed at Matthew and his sons. "Since y'all want to be Americans, my family wants to test your knowledge of our culture. The government made you take a test, but my family has our own test to see if y'all qualify to live here."

Trixie took over. "You get enough answers right, you live. You fail, you die. Questions?" She held up a finger, cutting off Mahdi, who had a question. "I lied. We don't answer questions." Trixie laughed at her rudeness.

After Tom winked at Tina, she asked the first question from memory. "Who won the 1996 NBA championship? This question is for Matthew."

"The Bulls," said Matthew, too cocky for Tom, seeing as it was only question number one.

"Even a blind squirrel catches a nut once in a while." Tina rubbed her hands together menacingly. Her comment made Tom smile. That was a saying he said frequently, something he learned from his mother. "The second question is for Mahdi. Who won the 1996 World Series?" Tina hummed the Jeopardy theme song.

"I... I... don't know." Mahdi stuttered, with tears in his eyes. He had the nerve to look to his father and brother for help.

"The Yankees," shouted Matthew, defending his traitorous son. Matthew was a better man than Tom. Had one of his sons betrayed him, he would have never forgiven them.

Tom and his family stood and booed Matthew. Tina jumped on Matthew and beat the dog shit out of him. She was forced to learn how to fight because she was surrounded by men. She was thin, but her punches hurt, as seen by Matthew squirming and screaming like a girl. Matthew's family was scared, but Tom's family cheered Tina on. To be fair to Matthew, Tom messed up by not saying they couldn't answer for each other. But life wasn't always fair.

Since Tina couldn't have all the fun, the family joined in punishing the Al-Amins for being dirty, rotten cheaters. Cord and Alex pounded on Mahdi and Amer while Trixie and Tom watched. Tom and Trixie didn't have to put in much work because their kids were eager to please them by showing how violent they could be. The Al-Amins hollered so loud that Tom turned on a radio to drown out the sounds.

"That's enough," said Tom to the children. He'd been so disgusted with Matthew answering the question for his son that he ended the game to move on to punishment. "Help me and your mama take the family to other rooms."

When the Sawyers rounded the corner, they entered an office. There were bookshelves against every wall. A desk fit for a king was covered in folders, and boxes covered most of the floor. Someone in the Al-Amins' family needed better organizational skills. Tom stared at the computer on the desk, wishing he had one. The only computer he used belonged to the library.

Tom said to the Sawyer kids, "Matthew will stay here with me and your mama. Find another room and do whatever y'all want with the others."

"You fuckers. Don't harm my children." Matthew lost his mind and wouldn't stop yelling.

Matthew had every right to go off, because he'd have it easy being with Trixie and Tom. His kids wouldn't fare well. Trixie and Tom's kids showed no mercy. Alex wasn't gay, just like Tom wasn't. Alex loved to punish men to show his strength. Cord never had sex with men, but he enjoyed doing strange things to people, and he'd had his way with a few female victims.

Once the Sawyer kids left, Tom and Trixie undressed and untied a battered Matthew. Although he tried to fight back, they overpowered him. While Trixie massaged Matthew's body, he grew an erection. His workers had been right about him; he was a pervert. The man's life was in danger, and his cock was hard. While Trixie violated Matthew, Tom watched.

Not long after, an outspoken Trixie screamed at Matthew, "Your wife is glad she's dead. Yuck!" She got up from the floor and stood next to Tom.

"You know nothing about my wife, whore." Matthew had lost all sense.

"Watch your mouth when talking to my wife." Tom kissed Trixie before he gave Matthew what he deserved.

After Tom finished, Matthew cried, "Get the hell out of my house. What more can you do to me? You've taken my manhood and dignity."

"One more thing and we'll leave." Tom fastened his pants.

Five minutes later, Tom and Trixie were the only ones alive in the office. They wiped down everything they'd touched.

In the living room, Alex and Cord wiped down as well.

"Where's your sister?" asked Tom. The boys knew never to leave her alone. Anything could happen.

"She wanted to take out some anger on those boys. Me and Cord had our fun and were done. Cord used his cigarette lighter again." Alex laughed. "Burn, baby, burn."

"You know the rule about your sister. Those two rich brats could've gotten loose," said Tom.

Tom and Trixie ran to the back of the house. They opened the door past the office to an empty bathroom. There was only one other room on the floor. Trixie opened the door and gasped before running out. She couldn't bear to see what Tina was doing to Mahdi and Amer. Far from naïve, Tom knew his daughter would someday have sexual desires. Yet, he expected her to wait until marriage: one man and one woman. Not one woman and two men. The only thing he wanted to see his daughter do with her mouth was talk, eat, and drink. The only thing she should've stroked in his view was a kitty cat. He'd never get this image out of his head.

Before Tina stood, Tom yanked her up and shoved her against the wall. Tom said, "You want to be a whore like your grandmama?" When she didn't respond, he let her go. She could be stubborn like her mother and his mother. She was his baby, so he refused to fuck her up, but he had to scare her. "If you ever do something like this again, I'll—" He stopped himself. "Get out of my face." He let her go. After she stormed out of the room, Tom stayed behind with Mahdi and Amer, who had defiled his baby girl. Not long after, Tom was the only person alive in that part of the house.

Back in the living room, Tom walked in on Trixie lecturing Cord and Alex for disobeying the rules. For added punishment, Tom made the boys clean the room at the back of the house.

Before leaving the home that once belonged to the Al-Amins, the Sawyer family stole money, food, Halloween candy, and anything else they could shove into their Halloween bags and pockets.

It would've been another glorious Halloween had Tina not ruined it for Tom. During the ride home, he kept getting flashbacks of what she'd done to those brothers.

12

BRANDY

Brandy slapped her hand on the dining room table. "That's what Tom gets. His daughter was a hoe. She didn't care that the boys were brothers. You write some freaky shit." Brandy liked the story but didn't know why. Maybe it was good. Or maybe she hadn't expected Carlotta to think of something like that. Either way, Brandy wanted to know the ending.

"I appreciate you for listening, seeing as I had to stop a few times to check on the food. But you misunderstand Tina. She wasn't a whore. Just a young girl who had sexual needs like everyone else in her family."

"Whatever. Tina was a hoe. Have you finished the ending?"

"We'll have to agree to disagree about Tina. I haven't written the ending because I know what happens and it ain't nice."

"Are they going to get caught and have a shoot-out with the police?" Brandy wished death on the main characters because they were evil.

"You'll have to wait and see."

After locking Carlotta in her room, Brandy sat on the bed in one of the guest rooms and argued with herself. She needed to call her daughter, but she didn't want to. However, she forced herself to video call. After explaining to Braelynn's foster mother why she'd had no contact, the woman offered to let Brandy take Braelynn trick or treating. She graciously accepted.

When Braelynn joined the video call, she stared blankly at Brandy and didn't speak. This was what she deserved.

"I love you, baby," said Brandy. "What have you been up to?" Humiliated, she held back tears when her daughter failed to respond.

The foster mother interjected, "Braelynn, you hear your mother talking to you. Tell her what we did today."

"You bought me a Halloween costume." Braelynn looked at her foster mother, refusing to make eye contact with Brandy.

"Tell your mother, not me."

Braelynn cried, "She's not my mommy! You are." The little girl ran off camera, her foster mother in tow. As she held back tears, Brandy couldn't be mad that her daughter wanted nothing to do with her.

The foster mother returned without Braelynn, "I'm sorry. She's refusing to talk. We'll see you on Halloween. Me and my husband will talk to Braelynn, so she'll expect you."

"I appreciate you," said Brandy before ending the call. She didn't know what she'd do if Braelynn refused to go with her trick-or-treating. She didn't want to force her, but she couldn't allow her child to get in the habit of not spending time with her.

An hour later, in the living room, Carlotta watched *Bonanza* while Brandy scrolled on her phone. When a text came through from Aunt Sheila asking about their well-being, Brandy deleted it. Her aunt was dead to Brandy, so she blocked her.

There was a knock at the door. Through the peephole, Brandy saw the delivery person drop off the groceries. After the guy drove off, Brandy got Carlotta's order. Brandy had previously used Carlotta's phone and money to make the purchase. Carlotta couldn't be trusted with her phone.

Zane entered the house without speaking and rushed upstairs like he had to use the restroom. Soon after, he screamed, "What the fuck? Brandy, come here, now!"

What happened now? When they got to the bedroom that Zane and Brandy shared, Brandy couldn't believe her eyes. All the new clothes that Zane brought were shredded on the floor. On the wall, someone spray-painted a message. *I'm not here to hurt you. I'm here to kill you.*

Brandy didn't know why, but she looked to the other two for answers. But how would they know anything? Carlotta had been at Brandy's side the entire day, and Zane had been at work. No one had entered the house. "I don't know who did this. Carlotta was with me." Brandy paused, contemplating how this could've happened, under the weight of Zane's accusatory gaze. Shortly after, she said, "Hold on!" She pointed at Carlotta. "This bitch did it. Tell me where the secret door is in your room!" Done playing with Carlotta, Brandy backhanded her.

To her astonishment, Brandy was met with a fierce glare from Carlotta, who then aggressively charged at her. Zane jumped in between the two to stop the fight. Behind him, Brandy threatened Carlotta, who looked unbothered.

"Chill the fuck out, you two." Then Zane said to Carlotta, "I'm trying to work with you, but you're making it hard. How are you getting out of your room?"

Carlotta sat on the bed with her legs crossed, looking dainty instead of behaving like the pitbull she was a second ago when she attempted to fight Brandy. "I'd forgotten about it until now, but last year, someone broke in several times. I never saw the person, but they'd steal food and spray paint the wall, saying they weren't here to hurt me."

"You ain't think it was important to tell us?" asked Zane, staring down at Carlotta.

"Don't believe her," Brandy cut in. "She'll say anything to keep us from finding her secret doors."

Carlotta shrugged. "I can see why y'all wouldn't believe me, but it's the truth. Like I said, I had forgotten about it."

Zane grabbed Carlotta's arm, which pleased Brandy. Finally, he wasn't playing nice with her. They all went to Carlotta's bedroom. Brandy and Zane knocked on every wall, searching for the hidden door, but found nothing.

Something was off, and Brandy wouldn't let Carlotta rest. Brandy asked, "How did the person break in last year? And how did they break in today with both of us here? Tell us the truth."

"I don't know!" Carlotta had too much bass in her voice.

Why had Zane stopped Brandy from whooping Carlotta?

Zane tried a gentler approach, "You never wondered how the person was getting in and out of your house? Did you find broken windows? Maybe they got a key. Could be a maintenance man if you got one."

Frustrated, Carlotta sat at her desk and rested her head in her hands. "Of course, I wondered how the person got in, but I could never figure it out. They never harmed me, so I let it go."

"You never called the police?" Brandy eyed Carlotta, not believing this story.

They had gotten nowhere with Carlotta, who claimed she disliked the police, so she never called them. Zane and Brandy needed to get out of that house for a few hours to think. Before leaving, they left a bucket with Carlotta in case she had to use the restroom.

***

Sometime later, they shopped for inexpensive clothes to replace the ones destroyed by the mystery person. They'd have to leave Carlotta's home sooner than expected. The rats were problematic, and now someone threatened to kill them. Had they known how the person broke into the house, they could've gained the upper hand. But not knowing made them easy targets.

The more she thought of it, the more Brandy never wanted to see Carlotta or her home again. She tried convincing Zane to go to a motel, and they could figure out a new plan in the morning.

"We ain't losing all our money on hotels," Zane said. "Just make sure you always have your gun on you, and don't get too comfortable with Carlotta. We need to stay with her for two more months, tops." Zane had some nerve to tell Brandy not to get too close to Carlotta when it was he who ate her food and watched TV with her.

"Two months?" Brandy stopped pushing the shopping buggy.

"I'll be in barber school and doing gig work. The loan officers will have no choice but to give me a loan for our house."

"Two months and that's it. I was thinking today about what I might do. Learning how to do tattoos sounds interesting. After Halloween, I'll see what I need to do to start as soon as possible."

"That's positive. And you called Braelynn." Zane smiled. "I talked to her today, too."

Out of embarrassment, Brandy held back the part about Braelynn dismissing her. While in the checkout line, Zane called Sherita, and she agreed the boys could go trick-or-treating with Braelynn if Zane bought them costumes.

Back in the car, they agreed that buying a second car would be a good investment, considering their schedules would change. Life was going in the right direction. They would no longer be just gig workers. They'd have careers. The next step was simple: find the one who threatened them... and return the favor, slowly.

13

BRANDY

Against Brandy's wishes, Zane pulled up to Sherita's apartment unannounced. When they parked, Sherita was on the other side of the street, hugging a good-looking older man while the kids played in the yard. When Sherita noticed Zane, she let go of the man. It was too late for her to pretend like she wasn't snuggled up with him. Zane saw it, and all hell was about to break loose.

Before Zane got out of the car, Brandy grabbed his arm and said, "I know you want to do something to them, but if you do, she won't let you see the—"

Pulling away from her, he exited the car, popped the trunk, and got the bags with the kids' costumes and candy. He walked to the apartment while Sherita wrapped things up with her sugar daddy.

Brandy stayed in the car, wondering how things would play out. She had been certain Zane would've fought Silver Fox or threatened to shoot him, but he hadn't. Zane's boys ran to him and embraced him. His kids were forgiving, which gave Brandy the faith that Braelynn would forgive her too.

Sherita approached Zane and their kids. To stop him from repeating what he'd done the other day, Brandy got out of the car. If needed, she'd take the children into the house while their parents argued.

"I got a man and I don't owe you any explanations," said Sherita, waiting for Zane to object. "We have kids, that's it."

The poor boys looked nervous.

Zane's response was nonchalant. "Do what you want. If you keep my kids safe, you and me won't have problems. But the moment one of your niggas step out of line, you and they will have a problem."

Judging by the stunned silence and wide eyes, Zane's calm response had caught everyone off guard.

"So, you not mad?" asked Sherita, who seemed like she wished he were.

"Nope." He faced his sons. "I'll be back on Halloween. Be good."

Sherita's mouth was wide open. Brandy realized at that moment that Sherita didn't want to be with Zane, but she needed him to want her.

Not long after, Brandy almost pulled the car over because Zane freaked out. He cussed and beat on the dashboard, showing his true feelings. "That bitch got an old nigga around my kids! I don't care who she's with; she'll forever be mine. The only reason I didn't spaz out was because of what you said about the boys not needing to see me and they mama like that."

Finally, he had listened to her. She wasn't dumb after all.

Zane stared out the passenger's side window and then turned around to face the back of the car. "Yo, that truck is following us."

"They've been behind us a while, but I ain't think nothing of it."

"Make a left."

When she made the turn onto the residential street, the red truck followed. At Zane's direction, she made a right at the stop sign. The truck followed that turn, too. Enough was enough—they both pulled their guns.

It was too dark to see who was driving. Two men sat in the truck, but their faces were shadows, their identities unclear. Brandy took the next right, steering the car down the roughest street in Miller—a battered stretch of Gary lined with broken pavement. The car bounced hard, jolting over one cratered pothole after another.

"Of all the streets, why did you choose this one?" Zane questioned.

"We have to shake whoever is in the truck." Brandy looked out the rearview mirror, assuming the truck driver would leave. No one in their right mind drove down that street. Slow speeds couldn't prevent tire punctures.

As she looked out the rearview mirror, the driver of the truck drove at a normal speed, unconcerned with the potholes.

"I'm done with this." Zane shot at the truck but missed.

"What the hell are you doing?" Brandy snapped. The road was empty—for now. But that could change in seconds. She wasn't about to risk prison time because Zane couldn't control his trigger finger.

"Drive." Zane fired another shot and rejoiced when the truck's front window cracked.

Whoever the person was driving the truck wouldn't give up. The truck sped up and rammed into the back of Brandy's car, causing her gun to hit the floor. Before Zane could let off another shot, the truck slammed into them yet again. Brandy's car ran off the road into the forest. Fortunately, she braked before colliding with a tree. The truck's driver honked but stayed out of the forest.

Shaken up, Brandy started the car, put it into reverse, but it didn't move. After ensuring they were both okay, Brandy called AAA. Then she and Zane exited the car with guns in hand, inspecting the car. The rear wheels were buried in soft dirt, and the back bumper—bent and sagging—hung over the brush's edge. No way could they get the car unstuck without help. Guns raised, they pushed through the woods, eyes sharp as they neared the road to confirm the truck had left. They had never killed anyone, but both agreed that if they saw those two who ran them off the road, they'd shoot first and ask questions later. The truck was nowhere in sight. Just silence, and a stretch of empty road.

Why would someone follow us? We haven't done anything... lately.

She and Zane had once followed shoppers or ATM users just to rob them—they knew the signs. But nothing about her car stood out now. They hadn't spent big. They hadn't pulled cash. No one should've had a reason to follow them. At least, not to rob them.

While they waited for AAA, Brandy and Zane stayed alert, eyes scanning their surroundings, nerves tight. They tried to make sense of it all. Who was after them? And why? Maybe it was someone from high school—grown people held grudges over dumb things. Or maybe it was recent—someone they'd rubbed the wrong way in an argument.

They didn't exactly keep their opinions to themselves.

When the tow truck arrived, the driver got them back on the road, replaced a shredded rear tire, wrapped the bent bumper with thick straps so it wouldn't drag, and handed them a bill—the last thing they needed. The car looked like hell, but it would roll.

***

Back at the house, Brandy and Zane tried relaxing downstairs. Zane read Sherita's message, saying she'd forgotten to tell him her mother was doing much better. That was good news to Brandy, but she knew Sherita had only given Zane an update because she wanted his attention. Women were so predictable.

Reaching Carlotta's room, they unbound her so she could empty her bucket. When she returned from the restroom, she surprised them both by offering to help clean their room. Brandy accepted—though she had no proof, she was certain Carlotta had played a part in what happened. Zane, softer than Brandy, said he'd repaint the threat spray-painted on their wall another day.

Brandy was tired. She climbed into bed with Zane and Carlotta who watched Westerns and ate popcorn. Brandy wouldn't sleep alone in the guest room after everything that happened. Before drifting off, she asked Zane to wake her when he was ready for bed. She barely slept, disturbed by Zane and Carlotta's laughter and movie quotes.

When she awoke, it was morning. Zane hadn't had the decency to wake her, which meant he slept in Carlotta's room, too. Carlotta and Zane sat on the bed eating pancakes, eggs, and sausages. Why was Zane so nasty?

"Try this." Zane stuck a forkful of pancakes into Brandy's face. Sensing her irritation, he removed the fork. "More for me and Carlotta, then." Carlotta and Zane toasted their glasses of orange juice.

After Zane ate, he and Brandy locked Carlotta in the room so they could bathe. It annoyed her when he told her he had stayed in the bathroom earlier while Carlotta had her bath. He tried convincing Brandy that it was innocent. But Brandy knew the truth. He hadn't woken her for a reason; he wanted to be alone with Carlotta.

Brandy glared at Zane, seated across from her in the tub. "I got my eyes on you, nigga." Her tone was sharp, but it cracked the moment her gaze dropped to Zane washing his dick. "My eyes are on something else, too." She reached for his manhood, but he caught her wrist, gently pushing it away.

"That was a one-time thing." Grabbing his dick, he said, "Is this why you are so concerned about Carlotta?"

"You had sex with her or got some top. Is that why you don't want me to touch you?"

He ignored her, stepped out of the tub, and dried off, leaving Brandy behind.

She pointed at his feet and shouted, "There goes a rat!"

Zane yelped, dropped his towel, and spun in panic. "Where? Where?"

"Here." When he turned, she flipped him off. Payback. He'd warned her not to screw up—then played house with Carlotta.

He stormed out, slamming the door behind him. Brandy stayed in the tub, fuming. She should've been the one slamming doors.

***

Against Zane's advice, Brandy went out alone for fast food. They still didn't know who had been after them, but she was starving—and what were the chances it'd happen again? As she waited for her order, she kept checking her surroundings, watching her back just in case. No one approached her. The only annoying part was people staring at her busted-up car.

Upon her return home, she entered the living room and could've sworn Zane and Carlotta held hands on the couch. Even if they weren't, they sat too close to one another. When Brandy tried making room to sit between them, Zane told her to move. What was so special about Carlotta that she held Zane's interest?

After the movie *Pride & Prejudice* ended, Carlotta said, "I finished the ending of my story. Can I read it? Pretty please?" Her begging annoyed Brandy. Everything about Carlotta irritated her.

Although Brandy wanted to know the ending, she said, "Zane hasn't heard your story, and I don't want you to start over from the beginning." She would do anything to stop Zane and Carlotta from bonding further.

"I've heard her story," said Zane. "She's good at what she does."

When had Carlotta had time to read to Zane? Those two woke up earlier than Brandy. Who knew what they did when she was asleep?

Carlotta turned the lights low, claiming she wanted to set the mood. Tomorrow was Halloween—what better time to read a horror story? She and Zane sat side by side, leaning in as the room fell into a soft, amber gloom. Brandy sat alone in the armchair, scowling at the two of them.

Carlotta opened her notebook and began to read, her voice slow and dreamy in the dim light. A rat darted from the dining room into the kitchen. Brandy didn't flinch. Normally, she'd be halfway up the chair. But not tonight. Not with Zane and Carlotta practically on top of each other, laughing like she wasn't sitting right there.

14

CARLOTTA'S STORY

2019

MUCH HAD CHANGED FOR *Tom and his family. They no longer broke into homes, because so many people had cameras. That disappointed Tom, since there were people on his list who deserved death. However, the family lacked nothing since they continued robbing to support themselves.*

He was proud of the parenting he and Trixie had done. The kids always lived within a mile of Tom and Trixie. Alex, age forty, lived alone since he often picked up random women at the bar and brought them back to his place. Although Tom settled down with Trixie when he was young, he didn't judge his son's lifestyle because the family stayed on the move. One day, they'd settle down so his boy could have a wife and kids. For all Tom knew, Alex might've had kids throughout America as much as he spread himself around. Tom hoped that wasn't true because no son of his would be a deadbeat.

Tina and Cord, both thirty-eight, had lived together in a committed relationship for years. Because the family feared judgment, Tina and Cord's relation was kept secret. The family found the cousins' romantic relationship beautiful. They would raise beautiful children with the right values. People in the past did this and were perfectly fine. Cord and Tina, blessed with good genes, would pass them on to their kids. Up to this point, they had been unsuccessful in their efforts to have children. Because the family was always moving, doctors couldn't determine what was wrong with them.

Tom often told his daughter to let out all her aggression before she had kids. That girl was feisty and would spit on or hit any woman who looked at Cord for too long. Tina never met a woman who could get the best of her in a fight.

Over the years, the family met a few decent people. That surprised Tom, who believed most Americans were full of shit. The family's friends were people whom Tom had beaten while gambling. Tom was an expert at hustling others out of their money or material items. He was a good talker, so it was nothing for new friends to extend invitations to the family whenever they passed through their towns and cities. This worked well for the Sawyers because they didn't have to sleep at rest stops or hotels if they were passing through a place.

Tom and his wife, Trixie, sat in their truck on a scorching afternoon at a convenience store in Milwaukee, Wisconsin. The kids were in Alex's truck, which was parked next to Tom and Trixie's vehicle. Since the family had more belongings these days, it was better that they traveled in two vehicles. The family had traveled extensively because Tom wanted them to explore the beautiful country they lived in. That was what brought them to Wisconsin.

After the last customer left, Tom and Trixie shared a quick kiss before putting on their masks and pulling out their guns. They left the truck, leaving the children outside to keep watch. Getting caught didn't worry Tom because their vehicles had stolen plates, and they were leaving Wisconsin after this job.

When Trixie entered the store, she said to the cashier, "Give us all the money and you'll keep your life. Is that clear?" Trixie looked hot in her shorts that showed off her meaty thighs.

The cashier appeared annoyed. This wasn't his first robbery. "Get the hell out of my store. I'm sick of being robbed, and it stops—"

"Shut the hell up and give us the money." Tom shot his gun at the ceiling. "Or the next shot won't be a warning."

When the cashier didn't move, Trixie jumped over the counter. Tom screamed when the cashier grabbed a gun from under the counter and shot Trixie in the chest. She fell forward and landed on the cashier's chest. This couldn't be happening. Would his wife make it through this? Tom jumped over the counter as blood seeped from Trixie's body onto the cashier. In shock, the cashier shoved Trixie into Tom, causing Tom to drop his weapon. Wanting to save Trixie, Tom sank to the ground and pulled her down with him, letting her rest on his chest. Her eyes were open, but she was barely breathing. When she attempted to speak, nothing came out. It wasn't the day Tom had imagined. His long run of problem-free robbing had ended. He'd never forgive himself if Trixie didn't pull through.

It must've been the cashier's first time shooting a gun because he looked wide-eyed at Tom and didn't shoot again. Tom remained on the ground, not caring about his life. Everything that happened next moved in slow motion. The kids barged into the store, yelling and threatening the cashier while Tom held onto his dear Trixie, who passed away in his arms. He hadn't gotten to say he loved her. Or that he'd see her on the other side. Nothing. She was dead.

"Stay with me, baby. You can't leave me like this!" Tom tapped Trixie's face as if that would make her breath return to her lungs.

Shots rang out. The cashier's body jerked and slammed into the wall, sending cigarette cartons crashing to the floor. Tom couldn't feel joy—not even relief—that the kids had taken out the man who killed their mother. Grief stole that from him.

As he stared at the cashier, daring him to die, the man raised his gun—and aimed it straight at Tom's head. With Trixie still curled in his lap, Tom couldn't move. He was trapped.

So he did the only thing a man could do when death was just inches away.

He closed his eyes and silently wished his children a good life.

The cashier pulled the trigger.

"No!" Tina screamed.

And that was the last thing Tom ever heard.

15

CARLOTTA'S EPILOGUE

2019

WHEN TINA, CORD, AND Alex each put a bullet into the cashier's chest, Tina was certain the man would die immediately. To her surprise, he squeezed off one bullet before dying. That bastard shot her father in the head. Tina leaped across the counter and almost fainted upon seeing her parents lifeless on the floor. It was unbelievable that they didn't have a more dignified death; instead, they were taken down by a chubby, bald cashier who probably earned the bare minimum. Had the cashier not already been dead, Tina would've shot him once more.

She lay beside her parents, begging them to come back to her, but it was too late. How could she survive without Tom and Trixie? They'd always supported her. But now they were gone. She was tough as nails because of them.

Cord and Alex jumped over the counter, and they both cussed to keep from crying. Alex attempted to pick up their mother until Cord stopped him. Had it not been for Cord, Alex would've carried their dead parents out of the convenience store. Once Alex stopped shouting, he helped Cord talk Tina into leaving.

"We got to go, darling," said Cord. "If we stay any longer, we're going to prison."

Ignoring Cord, Tina remained still. How could she leave their parents dead in a city they were passing through? They had to bury their parents in Tennessee. That was their home.

When Cord saw that talking was getting him nowhere with Tina, Cord picked her up and carried her kicking and screaming to their truck, with Alex in tow. She settled down when she realized Cord was right. There was nothing they could do for their deceased parents. If only she hadn't chosen that convenience store, their parents would be alive. She'd never forgive herself. All day something felt off to her, but instead of taking it as a sign that death was imminent, she ignored the feeling. She'd never be careless again. Not only did she have her life to think about, but she also had to consider Alex and Cord.

Alex shouted, "We can't leave!" He reentered the store.

"Man, what are you doing? Get back here." Cord fastened Tina's seatbelt as Alex ignored him. "Damn it! He's going to get us caught. We gotta go." Once Cord got in the truck and started the engine, Alex ran out of the store dangling their parents' keys and wallets.

"I'll follow y'all." Alex got in their parents' truck and trailed Cord.

Sitting next to her love, Tina stared out the window while Cord drove in silence. All she could think about were their parents. Tina, Alex, and Cord didn't have a traditional childhood, but she never faulted their parents for that. Their family traveled often and packed light, which taught Tina to never care about material things. Her parents taught her how to fight, cuss, shoot a gun, and kill people with weapons or her bare hands. Most of all, they taught her the value of family. It was family over everything. She'd kill for the family. If the police ever caught them, she'd keep her mouth shut and would take a charge to prevent her family from getting charged. Normal Americans weren't as solid as she and her family were.

As Cord drove south, Tina thought about the many people she and her family had terrorized. She'd always loved their parents for ensuring the children took part. Since they often researched American history, Tina, Alex, and Cord were smart as hell. One time, Tina presented to her parents that they should learn about other nations' history to spice up their games, but her father had been against it. He had said, "Screw that. Ain't no other country as good as this one, so we'd be idiots to learn about them. We're who they're trying to be."

The only thing Tina ever regretted about her childhood was not being able to meet her sexual desires with the victims because her father was strict. She was certain her mother had sex with the victims. However, Tina never understood why everyone could do whatever they wanted sexually except her. All her father would say was that she couldn't be a slut like his mother. Tina never had the heart to ask why he accepted her mother sleeping with different people. Didn't that make her mother a slut? Tina never judged her mother. She only tried to understand the situation from her father's perspective. She intended to raise her children similarly to her parents, except she'd allow her daughter to decide her own sexual preferences.

Tina was unsure of their destination, and Cord likely was too. She gazed at him, then out the window, before deciding their next step. Her sole responsibility was keeping the family united. The loss of her parents was devastating, but she would draw strength from it. Whenever they made it back to Tennessee, they'd honor their parents. Afterward, Tina and Cord would have a child because it was what their parents would want them to do. First, they'd have to figure out what prevented them from having kids to this point. She and Cord owed it to America to create children who would further the country the founding fathers envisioned. If it was the last thing she'd do, Tina would make their parents proud.

16

BRANDY

Brandy spent Halloween morning in bed, still wondering who had tried to run her and Zane off the road. They were as clueless now as they'd been that day. She also stewed over Zane—and Carlotta. Carlotta had read her story aloud the night before, complete with a twist ending. If it were Brandy's book, the Sawyers would've gone down in a blaze of gunfire with the cops. Something gorier. Something final. Still, she had to admit, at least the parents got what they deserved.

When Brandy had suggested changing the ending, Carlotta waved her off. "I just write what the characters tell me," she'd said. To Brandy, that sounded like a cop-out. Carlotta loved her characters too much to give them what they deserved.

It wasn't Carlotta's dumb story ending that upset Brandy—it was Zane. He'd violated her trust. Last night, after she begged him to come to bed, he brushed her off. Said he'd be upstairs soon. She'd drifted off, half-angry, half-hopeful.

Then came the screaming. Carlotta's voice, loud, ecstatic. Calling Zane's name.

Brandy shot up in bed, her mind spinning. She had to be dreaming. Hallucinating. There was no way—no way—Zane would sleep with their hostage.

To investigate, Brandy had crept down the hall to Carlotta's room, where the door was closed. Sure enough, Carlotta screamed Zane's name and told him to do many sexual things to her. Brandy glimpsed Zane and Carlotta having passionate sex when she cracked the door. While riding Zane, Carlotta had on a black bonnet pilgrim hat. Brandy left the door open and went back to her room to cry after Zane called out Carlotta's name. Did she experience jealousy? She believed there had to be more to it, so she pushed the thought aside. Zane still held the title of her best friend.

Zane's actions hurt, because how could she trust him? It had been obvious that he liked Carlotta, but Brandy had let him convince her otherwise. Brandy and Zane were there for a mission, not pleasure. Had she done something like that, he would've fought her, but apparently his rules didn't apply to him. Zane having sex with Carlotta was worse than Brandy getting them thrown out of Aunt Sheila's house and out of the motel. To make matters worse, as soon as Brandy assumed the sexual escapades had ended, they started up again.

Halloween should've been a great day. She had plans to pick up Braelynn later, and Zane would get his kids, and they would all trick-or-treat together. She hadn't thought about getting herself a costume, but that didn't matter. Her only desire was for Braelynn to have a good time. Despite what Zane had done, she wouldn't allow him to ruin her day. In an hour, she'd get out of bed, take her medicine, and cuss Zane out.

Brandy lay in bed, the door shut. Then—bang—it slammed against the wall. Zane stood in the doorway, gagged and bound. A rope cinched his wrists, another looped cruelly around his neck, its end held by someone just out of sight. All Brandy could see was a white hand gripping the rope. *Carlotta?*

"What the h—" Brandy started, but the words stalled.

Zane snarled behind the gag—no words, just heat and hatred. She knew exactly what he'd say if he could.

As Brandy reached for her gun, someone kicked Zane through the door. He stumbled forward and hit the floor hard. Behind him stood a muscular white man—blond hair, cold blue eyes, and a surgically precise cleft chin. Brandy screamed. Was this the man who'd scrawled the death threat across their wall? Had he come to finish the job? Or was he here to hand them over to the cops?

The man let go of the rope around Zane's neck and said, "Surprise! Bitch, you go for that gun and my cousin will blow your brains out."

There's more than one?

A medium-built white man with brown hair swept to the back of his head came into the room dressed in a leather jacket. He pointed a rifle at Zane's head and said, "I see Wifey has unwelcome guests. I'd say nice to meet y'all, but I'd be lying."

Who the fuck is Wifey? Carlotta, that lying bitch. I knew I couldn't trust her. This whole time, I thought no one loved her. How did she have a man, and she never left the house?

Zane, in just his boxers, kept grumbling, so the muscular guy punched him in the gut and he fell. Despite her anger towards Zane, she sympathized with him, but was powerless to help.

"We can leave," said Brandy, covering her breasts. The muscular man's lip-licking made her uneasy in her flimsy nightgown.

"Shh." The muscular man placed his finger over his mouth while his cousin lifted Zane from the ground. "Why would we make you and your friend leave?" He pointed at Zane. "Y'all like freeloading, so you two should stay a while."

As if something were funny, the medium-built man laughed. Something about the two men didn't seem like they were big on calling the police. They looked like they handled their own problems. It was something Brandy sensed because she'd been in the streets for years. She tried to convince herself otherwise. Maybe the men looked rough, but that didn't mean they wouldn't call the cops. Once Brandy got released, she wouldn't stop until she made Carlotta pay. She considered the additional time she'd spend away from her daughter. Braelynn and her foster parents would think she was a flake when she didn't show up to take her daughter trick-or-treating. But they'd be even more disappointed when they discovered she and Zane were in prison. Hopefully, the foster parents wouldn't tell Braelynn the truth. Brandy didn't know her legal rights. Could the foster parents adopt Braelynn if Brandy spent years in prison?

The muscular man snapped his fingers in Brandy's face and said, "Earth to freeloader. Now's not the time to zone out."

Emboldened, she said, "I don't have to answer you. I'll wait for the police."

The man chuckled, low and mean. "Who said anything about the police?" Then he yanked Brandy off the bed by her hair.

The medium-built man laughed and said, "In the words of *N.W.A.*, 'fuck the police'. Ain't that right, Dante?"

Chills ran down Brandy's spine. If the police weren't coming, what did this mean for her and Zane? Would they die and never see their loved ones again? The chances of that happening were small. Carlotta wasn't a murderer. The two men standing in front of Brandy seemed tough, but she imagined it wasn't easy getting rid of one body, let alone two. She rationalized the men were scaring her and Zane, and the police would be there any moment. Then she considered the fact that the guy pulled her by the hair, and her head ached. Someone making a citizen's arrest wouldn't do such things. Would they?

"Let me go," Brandy said, struggling against Dante's grip. "We have money." Dante released her—not out of mercy, but calculation. She stepped beside Zane. He didn't speak, but the set of his jaw, the way he shifted closer—Brandy could read him. If he could protect her, he would.

"We don't need money. You can't have too much of it since you took my honey hostage to stay here for free. We've broken into houses plenty of times, so I'm not judging you for that. But I am judging you for freeloading."

Where was Carlotta? Brandy expected her to pop out at any moment, but she didn't.

"Roderick, don't waste your time talking to her. She's a dead woman."

At that moment, Brandy was no longer in denial. The police weren't coming. She and Zane were in trouble. She had to save them. It was she, after all, who suggested taking advantage of Carlotta.

"We won't tell anyone about this," she suggested in a forced, neutral tone. "Beat us up and then let us go. Y'all will never see us again."

"I'm done talking." Dante yanked Brandy's hair again and led her downstairs while she screamed. Not only did hair rip from her scalp, but her body also banged against each stair. What type of monsters had she and Zane encountered? The other day while shopping, she should've worked harder to convince Zane to get a motel.

Behind her, Zane and Roderick followed down the stairs.

Carlotta sat in the living room wearing what Brandy assumed was her Halloween outfit: gray jogger pants, a white t-shirt, and a blue bandana.

Although Dante had Brandy by the hair, Brandy couldn't help but stare at Carlotta.

Carlotta said, "Boo! What are you looking at? I dress like the rest of you boring people one day a year. Victorian clothing reminds me of the good old days." Carlotta motioned for Dante and Roderick to sit Zane and

Brandy on the couch. "I'll have you know I look damn good in my dresses. You could use some fashion help, but we aren't here for that."

"We were nice to you," Brandy lied. "You were just fucking Zane last night, now you want to kill us." Brandy stared at Roderick after snitching on Carlotta. He should've been angry, but he looked like he couldn't care less. Her plan to expose Carlotta backfired. Upstairs, he referred to Carlotta as Wifey. He should've been concerned. "Say something, Carlotta."

"I'm Tina." Tina shoved her finger into Brandy's forehead, and Brandy immediately made the connection, which meant the two men must have been Alex and Cord. "Carlotta is an identity I made up. I like to pretend. What can I say? I even had a fake ID made using the name. You call yourself telling on me? Me and my man have an understanding. I can't wait to kick your ass."

Wait. What the hell is going on? How could I have been so stupid to pick this house? Out of all the houses in Gary, I pick the one belonging to the crazy, murdering family. Me and Zane are dead for sure. But maybe not. The family in the stories only killed wealthy people. Me and Zane aren't rich. We might have a chance.

"Oh shit! Where's the popcorn and drinks? Dante, help me move the furniture," said Roderick.

After they rearranged the furniture to create a circle in the middle of the floor, Roderick and Dante sat next to Zane on the sofa.

Tina entered the circle and said to Brandy, "Step up, fatty." When Brandy hesitated to join, Tina continued, "You scared of little old me? Not big Brandy, who is always talking shit."

Brandy wanted to fight Tina. But she wasn't stupid. She'd never gone toe-to-toe with a White woman before, but she liked her odds. Still, beating Tina would paint a target on her and Zane's backs—Tina's family would see to that. So today, Brandy chose peace. She and Zane had kids to think about.

"I don't want to fight."

"Sis, this bitch is scared," said Dante, almost laughing with a crooked smile. He acted like he was about to watch naked women mud wrestle.

Tina flexed her muscles at Brandy. Brandy hadn't noticed how defined her arms were because she always wore fluffy clothes. Brandy pretended she wasn't scared by holding her head high. The images of what the family had done to their victims flashed across her mind. That would intimidate anyone.

"Fight or your friend dies." Roderick pointed his gun at Zane's head. "I've thought of several ways to torture him."

Dante grabbed his crotch and smirked at Zane. Zane let out a muffled curse, the gag silencing every word.

"I ain't never been with a man with vitiligo." Dante licked his lips. "Today might be my lucky day."

Fuck! Fuck!

17

BRANDY

Left without a choice, Brandy entered the circle to fight. Tina charged her and hit her in the mouth. As blood leaked from her lip, she understood she'd underestimated Tina. Who knew such a thin woman packed a powerful punch? Not only that, she was a White lady.

"Fight back." Dante threw a pillow from the couch, hitting Brandy in the back. Apparently, her recovery time had been too long.

"You thought we were kidding, Little Miss Brandy?" Roderick removed a cigarette lighter from his pocket. No one wore their jeans rolled up at the bottom these days. He must've been in costume. He removed the gag from Zane's mouth. Ignoring Zane's threats of killing him if he got loose, Roderick placed the flame against Zane's face and held it there. "You see what you're making me do?" said Roderick to Brandy as Zane hollered from the burning sensation.

The family laughed while Brandy screamed and covered her mouth in horror. Since knowing Zane, she'd never seen such terror in his eyes or heard him yell and plead for mercy. They were utterly powerless.

"I'll fight!"

Zane's screams were too much to bear. She'd do anything to spare him unnecessary anguish.

Roderick threw Zane to the floor and said, "You can't seem to sit still, so stay on the floor. You're worse than a four-year-old child. Stop acting like this is your first time getting burned with a lighter."

"That boy is weak," said Dante, who lacked empathy.

Brandy and Zane had done some scandalous things, but they'd never burned anyone. They had hearts.

Defeated, Brandy blocked her face with her fists. If Tina wanted a fight, Brandy would give her one. To prevent Tina from getting the best of her, Brandy ran to Tina and threw several punches. A few landed, but none did any damage. As if she were an entertainer, Tina waved at her family instead of blocking her face. Brandy's punches made her laugh. Unexpectedly, Tina's smile turned cold, then she let off uppercuts that dropped Brandy to her knees. Roderick and Dante laughed and hollered like they were watching a professional boxing match.

Tina taunted Brandy, "You're much younger than me and you let me beat you. I'm forty-three and pregnant."

This was all too much to process. Brandy wasn't as tough as she thought; pain in her stomach solidified that.

Tina is pregnant. By who?

Dante and Roderick hugged and congratulated Tina. Zane looked as confused as Brandy.

"Zane and I had sex all night and early this morning." A proud Tina rubbed her belly. "The dummy didn't wear a condom, and sure didn't pull out. I can feel his seed growing in me." She kissed Roderick on the lips. "Baby, we are finally gone be parents. I told you your fertility issue wouldn't stop us from having kids. Mama and Daddy are smiling down on us from heaven."

"I'm gone be a daddy." Roderick picked up Tina and swung her around.

"And I can't wait to be an uncle," Dante chimed in. "The Buchanan family name and our traditions will live on." Dante turned to Brandy, who prayed that God would take care of Braelynn and Zane's boys should anything happen to her and Zane. "You and your partner did some good, after all. When me and Roderick cut y'all clothes, locked you in the restroom, and ran you off the road, it was because we hated you. But y'all are alright in my book now." He addressed Tina, "You're going to have to make the trip back to Alabama so we can show respect to our parents."

Tina was a habitual liar. She said the family was from Tennessee.

"We'll talk about that another time, brother."

Tina could fight—Brandy didn't doubt that. But she was a coward. She'd probably never leave her house again. Ironic, really. Once, Tina had warned Brandy that the world was full of danger. But Tina and her family hadn't just witnessed evil. They'd helped build it.

Although she tried, Brandy couldn't determine how Roderick and Dante got into the house without her and Zane knowing. Her mind immediately went back to Tina's big announcement. Was it possible that Zane impregnated her? Brandy looked at Dante, wanting to ask him a question, but she wasn't sure she should.

Somehow sensing Brandy's confusion, Tina said, "I'll help you put the puzzle pieces together." She chuckled. "You and Zane aren't that smart." She looked at Zane. "I pray the baby gets my smarts." Then she focused on Brandy as she continued, "Despite searching my home, y'all never found my other cell phone. Since you asked the other day how I came to Gary, I'll tell you. After our parents died in the convenience store in Chicago, we came here to stay awhile with our parents' friend, whom we named The Old Man. I developed agoraphobia and refused to leave, which was fine with The Old Man, who had been lonely. I've been here since. The Old

Man died and left the house to my family. Roderick and Dante can't stay in one place too long, so they travel, visiting every so often."

Carlotta had lied about everything—even their parents. The tale of their tragic deaths in Milwaukee? Fiction. She'd renamed her brother, her cousin, even the family surname. But in all her scheming, she'd left one thing untouched—her own first name. Brandy wanted Tina to publish the book, hoping that Tina's mistake would lead to the family rotting in prison.

Roderick joined Tina on the sofa and said, "I'm staying home from now on, darling. These heathens could've done anything to you if we hadn't been close by in Ohio. And now you're pregnant, so you need the support."

Tina blew Dante a kiss. Every member of this family was crazy. Tina assumed she was pregnant without a pregnancy test, played make-believe, and she slept with her cousin, who had a broken dick.

Curiosity got the best of Brandy. "How did y'all break into the house?"

"Tina was right. You are stupid," said Roderick, shaking his head. "As the owners, we have keys, and this house has hidden doors. The Old Man was into conspiracy theories and other weird shit."

"I'm done talking," said Dante. "Time to play."

Bound and on the ground, Zane declared, "We ain't playing your games. Carlotta, Tina, or whoever her name is, told us how them games ended."

Tina stood and dug her gym shoe into Zane's back. She said to her family, "The game can wait. I'm hungry, and y'all ain't had my cooking in a while."

"I can eat." Roderick left the living room and returned with a rope.

When Roderick tied Brandy's hands and feet, she replayed memories with loved ones in her head. She and Zane wouldn't leave the house alive. Once the family ate, they'd kill them. She was sure of it.

18

BRANDY

"THIS AIN'T LOOKING GOOD," Zane said. "These niggas is gone kill us." When Brandy didn't answer, he added, "Look, I got some things to get off my chest."

"We'll make it out of here," said Brandy, not wanting to terrify Zane further.

Zane was persistent. "Think about it, Brandy. In the story Carlotta told, each time that family played them games, people died."

"What about our kids?"

"Let me say what I need to say before it's too late."

Brandy was taken aback by how quickly he shifted the subject, but she remained silent.

Zane cried, which took Brandy back further. She'd never seen him this vulnerable. "There's no easy way to say this..." Zane let out. "Please forgive me, but... When I was eighteen, I killed your mother."

Brandy's thoughts raced, but she couldn't speak. Her mother's murder had remained a cold case. Word on the street had been that her mother set up the wrong drug dealer and lost her life because of it. Brandy had never learned who that drug dealer was. Had she, she would've killed him. No seventeen-year-old girl should have to face losing her mom. Brandy still found it hard to fathom that her mother's killer left her body in the alley with a single gunshot wound to the head.

Here Zane sat, telling her that he was responsible for her mother's murder. Zane and Brandy didn't play like this, so even though it was hard to take in, he wasn't lying. How could her best friend do this to her? They'd always had one another's back. When she grieved her mother, he seldom left her side and stopped people from asking her questions that usually came when someone died. Although she had lost her mother, having Zane around made things easier.

This was all too much to take in. He looked at her, waiting for her to say something, but she couldn't. He had lived with her at her aunt's house, and they did everything together. They had plans to get better jobs so they could buy a house for themselves and the kids. That was why they took Tina hostage, so they could save for Zane's dream of owning a home.

No longer at a loss for words, Brandy screamed, "If they don't kill your Black ass first, I will! What kind of friend are you? I loved you, and this is how you return my loyalty. Why?"

"Shh…" Zane tried to soothe her. "Before they come in here and kill us both."

"Fuck them and fuck you. Why did you kill my mama?" Before he could answer, Brandy shouted, "Murderer!" If only she could kick and strangle him, but they were both tied up. Tina's beating had Brandy in pain, but she'd push past the cramping in her stomach if she could hit Zane. She no longer cared about what happened to her or Zane.

"Your moms set up P. Rico." P. Rico was a drug dealer who most people in their neighborhood feared. "People assumed it was your moms because of her reputation, and they had seen her in the neighborhood of P. Rico's stash houses before men broke in and stole everything and killed P. Rico's two good friends. P. Rico put a hit out on your moms."

"You killed my mother with no proof! She cooked for you, and she and Daddy let you stay at our house on the weekends when the group home gave you overnight passes."

Zane continued his story as if Brandy hadn't interrupted. "Because of all she had done for me, I needed proof. One night, when I stayed over at your house, I went through her things and found P. Rico's ring with his initials that someone stole from his stash house. He couldn't keep his reputation and let your moms live. She was a dead woman walking. Why would I let someone else get the two thousand dollars? That was my thinking. After I did it, I couldn't sleep, and when I did, I had nightmares."

Zane deserved to die. No apology or tears would ever make what he had done right. If he told her about his nightmares to make her feel sorry for him, it didn't work.

"So with the money you got from killing my mother, you bought that raggedy car you used to drive. Am I right?"

Zane nodded. "I know you hate me, but there were many people after your moms. I heard some things they had planned for her. Because I cared for her, I shot her once and left her body where someone could find her."

All this time, Zane led her to believe he'd never killed anyone. He'd been serious about murdering Carlotta. Brandy had never felt so sick. She needed to get away from him but couldn't. Tears rolled down her cheeks. Zane ruined her and Braelynn's life. Had he not killed her mother, Brandy's bipolar symptoms may have remained dormant. Her father might've never gotten cancer, and he'd be alive today. Braelynn would have more family around, and a better support system. If things were different, Brandy would've been a better mother because her parents could've guided her.

"One moment I'm depressed, the next I'm hypomanic. You were angry when the system took Braelynn and upset because I didn't spend enough time with her. Why stay my friend? You feel sorry for what you did." Not allowing Zane to respond, Brandy continued, "Buying us a house is your way of making up for what you did to my mother. You did something terrible, and you punished yourself by being my friend."

Although it was tough to accept, she'd spoken the truth. His silence spoke volumes. All this time he had been laughing at her when she called him her best friend.

"You're dead to me," Brandy announced. "I hope the family kills you first so I can watch."

Zane's expression was etched in remorse until it morphed into a look of accusation. "You're pissed. I get it. But don't act like you're innocent. You've done some fucked up shit to me too."

Was he joking? There was no way he could consider her actions of getting them ousted from two places equal to him taking her mother's life. Brandy was seventeen when he ripped her mother away from her. She relied on her mother to navigate the challenges of being a teenager.

Brandy let out a low, angry chuckle. "You win," she said bitter. "World's most treacherous friend." How had she never seen Zane for who he really was? "I hate you! I hate you!" she screamed, her voice splintering on the last word. If Tina and her family wanted a war over her going off on Zane—fine. Let them come.

Once Brandy stopped hollering, Zane said, "I would've taken what I knew about you to the grave, but since you're acting innocent, I'mma tell you about yourself." Zane would say anything to make himself feel better. Accountability wasn't his strong suit. "You messaged Sherita, telling her I was still in the streets. No one else who knows me has Sherita's Facebook information. I see how you look at me. The other night, if I would've asked you to suck my dick and for some pussy, you would've gone for it."

Brandy had created a fake account to message Sherita, and assumed no one would find out what she'd done. Her plan to have Zane for herself had backfired. But if Zane knew Brandy was to blame, why had he kept it to himself? What he said about the way Brandy looked at him was also true. He was more than her best friend; he was the love of her life. She never expressed her feelings because he never looked at her like he desired her. Ever since he met Sherita, she was the only woman he talked about. That was why his sleeping with Tina came as a shock. Lacking confidence, Zane never approached pretty women. Tina must've seduced him.

Whatever dessert Tina made filled the room with a sweet aroma, making Brandy's stomach growl. All things considered, now wasn't the time to think of food.

Brandy didn't answer Zane because, for one, his revelation embarrassed her. And he tried to manipulate her by making her believe she was just as bad as him. What she did was wrong, but he still was the worst friend ever.

"I'm not done," Zane said.

She braced herself. What more could he possibly know?

"Who is Braelynn's father?"

Oh shit!

"If you have something to say, say it." If Zane knew who the father was, she would die. She needed her strength to conquer Tina and her family. She and Zane shouldn't have turned against one another.

Zane twisted the dagger. "Braelynn is my daughter."

How did he find out?

"Oh, I was drunk," Zane glared at Brandy. "But not drunk enough to forget you riding my dick." Brandy's breath hitched, she wanted to look away, but couldn't. "You raped me," he said. "That night—I thought I was fucking Sherita. The next morning, I knew it was you. Then you lied about not knowing who Braelynn's daddy was."

She'd felt horrible. That night, he'd said Sherita's name. Over and over. She hadn't cared. Wasn't in her right mind—that's what she told herself. But she didn't stop. She pushed forward, telling herself it was fine. But it wasn't. She knew that now.

Guilt got the best of her, and she could no longer ignore him. "She's yours. I wasn't taking my medicine when you and I had sex. When I got back on my pills, I was too embarrassed to tell you the truth. I knew you'd hate me. It's the hardest secret I've ever kept. Not even my father knew."

When Brandy suffered from depression, she regretted preventing their father-daughter relationship.

"You raped me! It's the first time I said it aloud. Don't blame it on having bipolar disorder. You did it when I blacked out because you wanted this dick and you took it."

That night, Brandy had been in a hypomanic state. She wasn't responsible for her actions. "I don't know what to say. None of what you said is worse than killing my mother."

"They gone kill us. That's why I told you about your moms, even though I knew it would hurt you. But you hurt me too. You pissed me off when our daughter was taken. I'm constantly calling Braelynn, but I can't visit because I'm not on the court order." Zane continued, "I wanted the house so all my children could be with me. You don't know how much it killed me that you and Sherita were pregnant at the same time. I got to lie and tell my other kids that Braelynn is their cousin instead of their sister. They'll never know their actual connection."

If she hadn't already felt bad, Zane mentioning her and Sherita having been pregnant at the same time made her feel disgusting. Not only had Zane taken one of the most important people in Brandy's life away from her, but she'd also taken Braelynn away from him and his boys. Tina and her crazy family would kill them. Braelynn and Zane's boys would grow apart, since the foster parents didn't know Zane's kids. And who was to say Braelynn would remain with the foster parents after Brandy's death? She could end up with new foster parents. Brandy had never understood why Zane focused on buying a house after he moved in with Aunt Sheila, but now it made sense.

Since Brandy was lost in her thoughts, Zane said, "I kept you around me to make sure you were your best self for our child. I wanted to be a barber to be a better father. I realized the way I was living was fucked up."

The family rounded the corner, interrupting their conversation.

Apron on, Tina announced, "Time to eat!"

Dante and Roderick moved them to the dining room table, where they released their restraints and compelled them to consume a meal: macaroni and cheese, BBQ-flavored ham hocks, string beans, hot water cornbread, and strawberry Kool-Aid. Brandy managed to prevent herself from throwing up. She couldn't lie—the food was good. But she couldn't stop picturing rats scurrying across the stove while it cooked. Zane ate like it was his last meal. With guns resting on the table, neither of them dared make a move.

Tina wiped her mouth and said to Brandy, "I knew you'd try my cooking one day."

I didn't have a choice, psycho.

Once the family had cleared the table, the game started.

19

BRANDY

Tina and Roderick cheered as Dante re-tied Brandy and Zane's hands.

"It's been so long since we played together," said Roderick to Tina. "I missed us."

"That is the sweetest thing I've heard in a long time." Tina kissed Roderick, which was disgusting since they were cousins, and first cousins at that.

"Save the mushy stuff for later," said Dante. He turned to Zane and Brandy and said, "I hear y'all know how the game works, but here's a refresher. Get the answers right, you live. Get them wrong," he chuckled, "and you die."

"How many can I get wrong?" Zane asked.

"We don't tolerate questions," said Tina. She pointed at Brandy. "The first question is for you." Brandy had been a poor student and a high school dropout. Death was imminent. "What was George Washington Carver famous for developing?"

Thankfully, Brandy knew the answer and let out the breath she'd been holding. "Peanut butter."

Everyone, including Zane, shook their heads.

"Damn, Brandy," said Zane, concerned. "Man, we dead. Our kids gone grow up without us." He pleaded with the family, "We'll do anything. Just don't take us away from our children."

Dante screamed at Zane, "Who told you to talk? Hell, I bet you don't know the answer."

As punishment, Roderick and Dante threw Zane to the floor and stomped him mercilessly.

Before Brandy could beg for Zane's life, Tina pushed her out of the dining room chair onto the floor. Tina said, "The answer is crop rotation methods."

The family wasn't playing fair. Brandy had gotten that answer right. While she lay next to Zane, it was difficult for her to watch him get beat up, so she closed her eyes. After finding out what he'd done to her mother, she should've rejoiced, but she had a heart.

Brandy couldn't focus on Zane—her mind was splintering in too many directions. One moment she was dressed; the next, she wasn't. Tina and Roderick had claimed her body in ways she hadn't consented to, hadn't prepared for. And Tina—the woman who should've known better, who should've defended the sanctity of being a woman—was the worst of them. Still, some quiet voice in Brandy whispered a question she wasn't ready to answer. *Was this karma?* Was this payback for that night with Zane? Even now, she couldn't say the word. *Rape.* That was what monsters did. What Tina's family did. Brandy wasn't like them. She was a good person. Wasn't she?

Brandy finally looked to Zane for sympathy. But there was none. Tears rolled silently down his face. When he caught her watching, he shut his eyes. She didn't blame him. Not for refusing to let her witness his pain. Dante had taken what he wanted from Zane—fulfilled the same twisted desires Tom once had with the family's other male victims. And just like that, Zane became another name carved into Halloween's long list of victims.

Minutes after she left, Tina returned to the room, armed with three machetes.

"Shoot me and leave me somewhere my kids can find me," said Zane, now that Dante had left him alone.

"Yes, please," said Brandy, not wanting to end up chopped to pieces. Zane had a point; a bullet was better than death by a machete.

Tina cut Brandy off. "Y'all are something else. You think it's right to beg for mercy when you two planned to kill me?" Tina handed machetes to her family. "I knew too much about y'all since you dummies didn't wear masks. And it didn't take a genius to figure out my life might end if my family didn't come home."

"We weren't going to—" said Brandy before Dante signaled for her to be silent.

Roderick and Dante sat them down into chairs. Though Brandy wasn't a praying woman, she asked God to protect Braelynn and Zane's boys. Considering all she had done, would God even hear her? Brandy and Zane had an agreement to kill Tina before they took over her house. However, she was not serious. She just discovered today that Zane had been. He murdered her mother, and potentially other victims Brandy didn't know about.

"Question two is for you, Zane," said Tina. Brandy had assumed the game was over. She didn't have it in her to think of answers, considering all that had happened and what more was to come. "What state did Kamala Harris represent before she was elected vice president?"

Zane had seen better days. The light had left his eyes. "D.C." It sounded like it pained him to speak.

The family erupted in laughter. They were cocky for people who likely looked up the questions and answers on Google. Brandy did not know the answer, but it must not have been D.C.

Brandy screamed, begging Tina to stop, but the machete was already in motion. She turned away, eyes clamped shut, sobbing. Zane's screams tore through the room and vibrated through her bones. Something inside her splintered. Then—a sickening thud. She opened her eyes. Tina stood over him, breathing hard, and swung again. The final blow.

Brandy screamed, "No! No! No!" as she realized there was no way to escape, feeling a sense of impending doom.

Blood was everywhere. Zane was dead. Brandy could only scream and tremble while Dante and Roderick celebrated.

Roderick stood over Zane's lifeless body, admiring Tina's work. "Tina's just made America safer," he declared.

Tina dabbed at the blood on her face with a napkin, acting as though it was perfectly normal. She turned to Brandy, who was howling through her sobs. "Next question," she said, as if nothing had happened.

Brandy had no religion to fall back on—just a single line of scripture lodged in her memory. She repeated it over and over again. "The Lord is my shepherd. I shall not want. The Lord is my shepherd. I shall not want. The Lord is my shepherd. I shall not want."

"You're a menace and you're praying," Tina laughed. "Answer this question right, and I'll keep you as my servant girl. I won't kill you. I promise." Tina was full of shit. Brandy wasn't the smartest, but she wasn't stupid. "Who made history as the first African American President of the United States?"

Dante said, "Too easy," as he quieted Brandy's screams with a swift slap.

Having witnessed what happened to Zane, Dante's slap barely fazed her. Brandy dissociated, no longer yelling. Memories of happy moments with

Zane flooded her mind, making her wonder about the alternate course their lives could've taken had she not stopped taking her medication. Dante drenched her with water, bringing her back to reality.

She shouted in surprise, "Ahh!" Brandy tried to focus on Tina's question, even though she was freezing and trembling from the water Dante had drenched her with. "Barack Obama," she said, barely above a whisper.

No one cheered when she got it right. No high-fives. She almost wished they'd end her suffering. Death had to be better than spending another moment with the Sawyers. *Will I be with Zane in death? I'll miss Braelynn. What I did to her wasn't fair—she didn't deserve it. God, I love her.*

"She accused me of hating Black people, but I guarantee you she doesn't know as much about Black history as we do," Tina boasted to Dante and Roderick. "I hate when people assume things about me. Our parents weren't racists, and neither are we. They believed quality jobs should be for Americans. The foreigners could get jobs as long as they didn't steal positions from someone born here."

While the family talked and remembered their parents, Brandy reflected on her love for Zane, wishing he knew how much she cared before he died. Despite the destruction of her family and her mother's death, she forgave him, realizing holding grudges against the dead was pointless. But had he survived, she questioned whether she could have ever forgiven him.

Tina smiled, knowing Brandy was doomed. Tina said, "Angela Davis became an iconic figure in the Civil Rights movement. What is one of her most notable contributions to the cause?"

Brandy, accepting her destiny, stayed quiet. She hated weak women—and she wasn't one. Zane's murder left her feeling numb. Her next words would've made him proud.

"Bitch, fuck you and your perverted family!" She'd see Tina and her family in hell. She cried as she carried on. "Rot in—"

Tina cut her off mid-scream, slammed her down, and stood over her, laughing—machete in motion. Brandy let out one final cry as pain and blood overwhelmed her. The family roared with applause and cheers as she faded. Tina just laughed, gaze locked with Brandy's, savoring every second of the kill.

Tina stepped back, blood dripping from her blade, admiring what she'd done to Brandy's body. A beat of silence hung in the air.

Then Roderick grinned. "Somebody get a body bag!" he shouted.

Dante began to clap. Slow. Measured. Then Roderick joined in. Then Tina. Until the room swelled with eerie applause—low and rhythmic, like the final cue in a stage production.

Tina smiled and bowed, her bloody hand on her newly pregnant belly. "Happy Halloween, family."

The family erupted in cheers.

"Happy Halloween!" Roderick and Dante shouted together, perfectly in sync.

EPILOGUE

THE FOLLOWING HALLOWEEN, TINA realized how much her life had changed. Roderick did what he said he'd do and stayed home with her. Dante went off on his own as expected. Tina signed up for online therapy last year to address her agoraphobia. Earlier this year, she progressed to meeting the therapist at the office. The road had been hard, but Tina endured it for the sake of her family. She had panic attacks when in public, but allowed them to pass and went about her day.

Roderick and Dante walked alongside Tina while she pushed a three-month-old Anna in the stroller. Tina and Roderick named their baby after their mother, whose real name had been Anna.

Anna wore a pumpkin costume for her first Halloween. She was the joy of her family. She looked like Tina but with yellow skin. Dante once asked Tina and Roderick if they were concerned their child would develop vitiligo, but they weren't. They'd love her no matter what.

After Tina killed her unwelcome guests last year, Dante and Roderick chopped up the bodies and spread them across the Midwest. Since Tina and Roderick were decent people, they took information from Brandy's and Zane's phones before destroying the devices. Tina periodically checked in on Zane and Brandy's families after their loved ones accepted her as an online friend. Braelynn still lived with her foster parents, who often posted pictures of her with hearts covering her face with them on vacations and holidays. Tina discovered that the foster parents couldn't show Braelynn's face online per court rules.

Sherita married a much older man, and Zane's children were a part of the wedding. Zane's boys appeared sad in the pictures, but Tina was confident they'd one day forget about their no-good father.

When Zane and Brandy disappeared, their families posted about them and shared photos, asking if anyone had seen them. Such posts decreased and eventually stopped when there was no trace of the two. Against Dante's wishes, Roderick and Tina occasionally sent money anonymously to Zane's boys. It proved impossible to send Braelynn's foster parents cash. The two would keep track of Braelynn and send her money once she turned eighteen.

The night Brandy and Zane died, Dante had been eavesdropping and heard Brandy and Zane arguing about Zane killing her mother, Brandy raping Zane, and Zane being the father of Braelynn. Dante didn't have kids, so he didn't understand the debt that Roderick and Tina owed Zane. Had it not been for Zane, Roderick, and Tina would've had to adopt. But now they had Anna, who was related to them both.

Dante and Roderick talked Tina out of publishing her short story. She eventually had to admit that changing more details in the story wouldn't suffice; someone might put the pieces together, and the family would still be at risk.

Her priority these days was getting used to being a mother and making her man happy. The family planned to visit Alabama next month to bury their parents' cherished American flags at a cemetery, and for Tina and Roderick to introduce Anna to her grandparents. Tina expressed gratitude for the positives in her life by kissing Roderick on the cheek. They'd honored their parents' wish to continue the lineage. The Buchanan legacy thrived. Anna would be brought into the tradition eventually—just not yet. She was still too young.

Thanks to Roderick, Tina, and Dante, Anna's childhood would be fun, just like theirs. At least, that's what they told themselves.

The End

AUTHOR'S NOTE

Thank you for reading my novella. I hope you enjoyed it. Please consider writing a review, no matter the length, as long as it reveals no spoilers. If you choose not to review, please leave a star rating at the very least.

Also by Samyra Alexander

ABOUT THE AUTHOR

Samyra Alexander, author of the popular and addictive series, *I Should Have Worn a Curtain*, has always flourished in the art of verbal story-telling. Samyra's love for reading ignited her imagination, inspiring her to write books in the genres of psychological suspense and psychological thriller.

Samyra's hometown is Gary, Indiana, but she now calls Los Angeles her home. With a doctorate in Clinical Psychology, she delves into mental health issues and their taboos through creative fiction. Samyra's passion for creating memorable characters that readers would love to strangle takes over when she's not working as a psychotherapist.

If you'd like to connect with Samyra, below is where you can find her.

Her website, where you may purchase signed copies of her books: www.samyraalexander.com

TikTok: tiktok.com/@authorsamyraalexander

IG: author_samyraalexander

Follow her on Facebook at Samyra Alexander Author Page

Email: tellsamyra123@gmail.com